SPACE WALRUS

Also by Kevin L. Donihe

The Traveling Dildo Salesman

The Flappy Parts

Night of the Assholes

Washer Mouth: The Man Who Was a Washing Machine

House of Houses

The Greatest Fucking Moment in Sports

Grape City

Shall We Gather at the Garden?

Walrus Tales (as editor)

SPACE WALRUS

KEVIN DONIHE

ERASERHEAD PRESS
205 NE BRYANT STREET
PORTLAND, OR 97211

WWW.ERASERHEADPRESS.COM

ISBN: 1-62105-028-9

Printed in the USA.

I'd like to thank:

Corey Welton
(for helping me mangle a Steve Miller Band lyric)

Ashli Carte
(for giving this a last-minute read, straight from China)

and

Nick Mamatas
(for his always welcomed feedback)

MASTER OF SPACE

The walrus sailed through the vacuum of space. He didn't need a suit or a breathing apparatus to survive. He didn't need to be connected to a line, tethered to some floating piece of tin. He was a Master of Space and a constant wanderer. But he was not homeless. The whole universe was his dwelling, and he intended to open its every door and enter its every room before his time was through.

His name was Space Walrus.

He had three hundred forty-one tattoos over 72.6% of his body, a few of those areas internal. He knew the percentage instinctually. There was no need for computation.

His favorite tattoo was of a walrus maiden, crying alone on a rock. She was his nameless, faceless soul mate, and she wept for him. He'd had many a lover, one just the day before, on an otherwise dry and inhospitable planet where he'd been called to destroy an invading Cyclopean army, but never had he lain with another walrus.

Someday, he trusted, his maiden would finally stop crying.

For the time being, Space Walrus decided to blank his mind and relax. He felt he deserved that much. A day without a mission was a rare treat, indeed.

With a single swoop of his tail, he sliced through reality itself. Space, he knew, had not only smell and taste, but sound, too. Space Walrus realized that the ancient ones weren't so far off when they discussed the music of the spheres. Opening his mouth, he allowed the essence of the cosmos to enter and infuse him. It was all the nutrition he needed.

His head tilted back.

He unleashed a sigh.

Suddenly, a beam of light enveloped him. He could see nothing but white.

He felt a strong pull. Space Walrus understood its source was the beam itself.

He struggled against the beam, but could not resist its influence. He was dragged down, inexorably down, to a ship of uncertain origin.

I AM WALTER

A cylindrical, walled space—slick and metallic—surrounded Walter. He tried to climb back towards the ceiling and the dark, star-filled hole he saw in his head. Still, his descent continued.

Upon reaching window-level, the walrus spotted Dr. Stephanie outside the chamber. Immediately, he felt lighter, but not so light that he could dream. Dr. Stephanie was his trainer and favorite human. Her body was thin and wispy, hair long and brown. Walter could only imagine what it felt like. His electro-fingers—attached to electro-arms, bolted permanently to his skeleton—were insensate.

Eventually, his flippers touched cold ceramic tiles. A door slid open. He flopped out of the chamber on flippers that felt like mush. Dr. Stephanie got down on her hands and knees. When Walter reached her, she enveloped him in a hug. "Great job!" she said, her body wrapped all around him.

He reveled in her touch and the feel of her skin against his, so unlike his own. "Thanks, Dr. Stephanie," Walter replied through the vocal-converter hardwired to his brain, his voice a digitized monotone.

She broke the embrace, but continued to kneel. "You looked like an angel in there."

"Really?"

"Yeah." She nuzzled him. "A big, special angel."

"I was having a nice dream," Walter turned from her, looked wistfully at the chamber. "I'd like to go back. Dream again."

"When?" Dr. Stephanie asked.

"Now."

She looked sternly at him, shook her head back and forth. "Excess sensory deprivation isn't good for you, Walter. But you'll be up there soon, I promise." Her expression softened. "Maybe next time, I'll join you."

Walter's brain sent impulses to his facial implants, stretching his features into a smile.

DOWN ABOUT GRAVITY

Walter's flippers and belly made slapping noises against the floor as he walked to his room with Dr. Stephanie. The sounds mocked him, made him feel earth-bound and fat. Never would his steps be like Dr. Stephanie's, so soft and unassuming.

He said nothing, just looked at the steel floor and then at the steel walls and ceiling. Everything was bright, shiny, clean and uninteresting. Spontaneously, he wished that a space beast might burst out from behind one of the doors and that his electro-arms might develop ray guns to deal with the interstellar threat.

"Why so down?" Dr. Stephanie asked. She seemed to sense all the emotions he thought were hidden.

"Gravity," he said, finally.

"You know, there's no real gravity here. The space station generates artificial gravity as it spins."

"Artificial gravity is still gravity," he replied. "It doesn't count unless I float."

From behind a nearby door, Walter heard an airlock start to open. Dr. Ron and his chimps were returning from a practice space walk. The walrus didn't want to deal with the doctor or his little brown bastards, so he hurried past the door.

Dr. Stephanie turned a bend in the hall. Walter relaxed and slowed his pace. "When can I practice in space, too?" he asked her.

She kept her gaze aimed down the hall. "I don't know, Walter."

"But—"

"It'll come in its own time."

One of the few things Walter remembered from his early training was Dr. Stephanie teaching him—more in actions than in words—the virtue of patience. He considered it a terrible virtue.

They stopped at his door. Finally, she faced him. "See you later, Walter," she said.

"Can you come inside, talk with me?" He willed his facial implant to form a plaintive expression. Manipulating her felt wrong, but it'd been weeks since they'd hung out during free time.

"No, not now. I'm so busy."

Walter's phony expression became genuine.

Though there was no day or night in space, it was simpler to speak in such terms. "I'll come back tonight to bathe you, okay?" Dr. Stephanie said.

The mere thought caused a frisson. "Don't forget," Walter replied. Silently, he cursed his implants. He hadn't intended to sound so demanding, but the vocal converter was the least reliable device hooked to his body.

The doctor didn't seem offended. She even stroked his head. "I won't," she said.

Walter leaned into her touch. When Dr. Stephanie withdrew her hand, the feel of it lingered on his hide.

She waved at him. "See you later, cutie."

WALTER'S REALM

Before settling down, Walter locked the door. Things felt cozier—more protected—with the latch fastened, and it wasn't as though he were locking Dr. Stephanie out. She had the master key and could enter whenever she wanted or needed.

Not that she wanted or needed very often anymore.

Taking a seat on his bed, Walter reminisced about the last time Dr. Stephanie had really hung out with him. The conversation had been great, but the subsequent role-playing had been sublime. Effortlessly, she became Princess Stephanie; he became Space Walrus, and together they explored a strange and foreboding world.

"Oooh, save me Space Walrus!" she'd said, as a squid-like space beast emerged from behind an orange rock to ensnare her. "Save me!"

Had it been a movie, climactic theme music would have soared. Just as he prepared to reach out, grip the tentacles and rip them from her—an act for which he might receive a kiss on the cheek—her phone rang and she had to go somewhere, do something. The alien world morphed back into his boring room; Princess Stephanie became Dr. Stephanie and Space Walrus became Walter. He hadn't role-played since.

From the outset, Walter suspected Dr. Ron had been on the other end of the phone. Dr. Stephanie had started talking about him more and more, and Walter knew that free time once spent with him was now being spent with the other doctor. But maybe her infatuation would pass; maybe Dr. Stephanie would see Dr. Ron for the prick that he was and deal with him only when necessary. Maybe it would just get worse.

Walter felt flustered. He wanted to stop thinking about this, but there wasn't much to see or do inside the 10x10 steel-walled chamber, though small touches had been added to make it homey—rugs on the floor and posters on the wall; his reinforced, low-lying bed had a pink comforter. A plush walrus was propped against a coffee mug on Walter's desk. Dr. Stephanie also encouraged him to watch movies, listen to music, and had supplied him with so many choices he'd yet to absorb them all. A training session, however, started in an hour. Music alone would have to suffice.

Walter moved to a touch-screen monitor and queued up a play-list of his current favorites. *Space Cowboy* by the Steve Miller Band wafted from ceiling-mounted speakers. "Some people call me the Space Walrus. Some call me the Odobenus of love," Walter sang as he returned to bed.

Next up: *Space Oddity*. Once, he had visualized himself as Major Tom, floating in a tin can—but that was before he understood the character's fate. Afterward, it had taken almost a month before he could listen to the song again without imagining himself forever lost in space.

Then came *I Am the Walrus*.

No, you certainly are not, Walter thought. Still, he liked the song—it was weird, hooky, but most of all, it rocked—so he didn't fault the human vocalist for being delusional.

More songs came and went. Losing himself in the flow, Walter began to feel a bit too relaxed. Dr. Stephanie would be upset if he slept through training, so he decided to get up and do the one exercise he could perform in his room.

He went to his desk, opened it and removed a sheet of paper. Unfolding it, he looked at the centerfold that seemed to stare back at him. He'd named her Betty. Supple and lithe for a walrus, she was the best looking animal he'd ever seen.

Dr. Stephanie had seemed strangely sly and said cryptic things when she presented him with the poster, like she knew—or even wanted—him to do what he wound up doing, sometimes multiple times a day. In retrospect, this embarrassed him. He imagined Dr. Stephanie somehow knew when he was pleasuring himself and often wondered if—like in other parts of the station—hidden cameras were watching over his room.

Walter returned to bed with the poster, which he placed on his pillow. Masturbation via electro-hands had taken some time to master—during one scary moment, he thought he might have severed his penis—but now he found the act preferable to awkwardly mounting or rubbing up against things in his room.

Stretched out on the comforter, Walter tilted himself sideways against the wall and gripped his phallus while staring hard at Betty.

He worked the shaft. His eyes started to cross. In his mind, he saw Betty lying on her back in bed, gauzy sheets bunched around her nude form. Walter approached her, ball-gag in hand. He had learned what ball-gags were from a particular movie. Dr. Stephanie probably wouldn't have let him see it had she known about that scene.

Mounting Betty, he plopped the ball-gag into her mouth and slapped his flippers against the back of her neck and head—two times, three times. He got harder, harder still, but deflated as guilt started to trickle in.

Dr. Stephanie had made it clear that men—even walrus men—shouldn't view females as mere sexual objects. They were to be cherished and admired, not beaten about the head with flippers.

The image of the ball-gag fell away. Instead, he began to wonder about her, who her friends were and what she liked to eat and talk about. What were her favorite movies, favorite songs?

Walter assumed he'd never know, but he could imagine. She liked horror films and punk rock. Though on the rebellious side, she was more inclined to wax philosophical than commit random acts of violence. Her favorite food was Mussels

Josephine, a dish she cooked like a pro. Her similarly aged friends harbored largely vacuous concerns, but Betty was into history and politics and was working on her second PhD. She hoped to have children, but not until she was ready.

In time, they would come to know and appreciate one another's quirks, get married, and on their honeymoon night in the Bahamas, her quick little kisses would pepper his body.

His penis began to re-inflate. "Oh, Betty," he moaned through his converter. "Oh Betty, I love you. Ooooh!" He stroked faster. "I love—*Ooooooooooh!*"

With that, Walter fell back onto the bed, exhausted yet smiling.

KIDNAPPED BY TRIMUNGULAGS

The beam had carried Space Walrus to a ship, past an airlock and into a vast hall. The walls were adorned with paintings and tapestries. Thick white columns towered every few feet, crowding the brightly polished walkway. Overkill in his eyes. He preferred to keep things simple.

He regarded his abductors—pale, skinny humanoids standing on stubby pillars of equal size, except for the central man, whose pillar was taller. Males were bedecked in gauzy pink robes, females in pale blue. All wore glittering sweatbands. Closer, Space Walrus saw how they emanated subtle blue rays from visible orifices.

Space Walrus opened his inner eye then, scrutinized these entities in a way that went beyond the mere visual. He peered deep into their souls. Indeed, at their innermost essences. They seemed a peaceful, studious sort, but Space Walrus didn't let his watchfulness slip. Perhaps they could cloak their true natures, throw up a screen that could deceive even his intuition.

"Hello, Space Walrus," said the man on the tallest pedestal, a wan, older sort, with a shock of gray hair that poked past a golden crown.

"You know my name?"

"We have been monitoring you for a while now."

"Perhaps you should mind your own business," he said.

The king lifted his hand, a placating gesture. "We needed to access your skills, but know that we are pleased with what we've seen." He gestured to a line of black, cube-like machines. "And with what our computers have indicated."

The king turned slightly. Space Walrus realized that the

blue light emanated even from his backside.

Two pillars to the right of the king, a brown-haired wisp of a man cleared his throat. He was the royal consort.

"It seems Our Princess, Stephanie, has been kidnapped by Trimungulags from the Bungulanugilarian Galaxy," he said. "They are mavericks, traders in flesh and bone. Anyone who comes into contact with them is almost surely doomed."

Space Walrus hadn't heard of this race. Odd. He thought he'd encountered them all.

The king continued, "We call them space beasts. We think it's fitting."

"And they're as fearsome as they sound!" shouted a random man in the hall.

The king glared at the man, then turned his attention to Space Walrus. "There's nothing we can do to help her; we are powerless—but you, noble walrus, are far from that. We are confident that you alone have the fortitude to defeat the Trimungulags and rescue her."

Space Walrus was likewise confident, but did not boast.

"So, will you accept this mission?"

"Need you ask?"

"Perhaps not. But know that it will not be easy. The Trimungulags deal with threats to their order in vile and unspeakable ways."

Space Walrus shrugged. "Not a problem," he said.

"They can turn a man inside out just by looking at him."

He remained unfazed.

"Seriously, they can do that."

"We've seen them," said another.

"So you all tell me."

"They can make a man's head turn and turn and turn, *but they keep him alive the entire time*," added the royal consort.

"I understand this happened in the past."

The king raised his hand. "Forgive us, please. We have utter faith in your abilities, but we want you to understand the risks."

18

"There are risks in breathing."

"I see." The king bowed. "May the great Crantonabula be with you forever, Space Walrus."

Space Walrus just nodded, having never heard of that god.

"But I hope your confidence doesn't prove your downfall."

"I appreciate your concern, but I just want to ask one thing before I go,"

"And that is?"

"Where's the shitter?"

The king looked embarrassed. "We don't do that, friend. At least not in the way to which you are accustomed."

"And that means?"

"The light you see. Well, it's our manner of defecation."

"Really?"

"Indeed. But we have cleansing rays that can take care of your problem."

"Don't worry about me; I'll make due."

With that, Space Walrus was off.

ZAPP THE CHIMP

Walter had dozed off. Only minutes remained until he had to be at the gym.

Quickly, he rolled deodorant beneath his flippers. He'd gotten it from the supply ship that had docked the week before—the first in three months.

Dr. Stephanie had told him he wouldn't need it; walruses didn't sweat. Still, it seemed right to apply the stuff—guys did it in movies—so, upon his urging, Dr. Stephanie placed the order for him.

Finally, he slipped on an orange sweatband and regarded himself in the mirror.

Atop his head was a rubber cap, also orange. Wires sprouted from it, wires sometimes connected to other wires, or machines. It couldn't be removed. Never had he noted anything like it on walruses in books or on TV. Once, it distressed him. Now, he thought the cap looked rather good, a touch roguish. The burnt orange color contrasted nicely with the pinkish gray cast of his skin.

Satisfied that he was ready as he'd ever be, Walter left the room. He traversed the largely featureless hall, turned a corner. There, Dr. Ron's chimps—all five of them—were clustered just outside the door to the science gym, wearing matching jogging shorts and tanks tops. Walter felt naked in his sweatband, but workout gear wasn't simpatico with his build.

Zapp—the de facto chief—leaned confidently against the wall, one foot propped on it, leg crooked. Most other chimps were lost in the moment, and in Zapp. Walter had no idea why they fawned over him. Perhaps chimps admired assholes.

Walter lowered his head, avoiding eye contact as he neared.

"You lookin' at me?" asked Zapp.

Walter bristled. Zapp's voice sounded so smooth and natural, not at all like the walrus' flat, electronic tone. The chimps had all gotten upgrades almost a year earlier.

Walter said nothing. Perhaps they would keep quiet if he didn't engage them.

"Damn, you must weigh a thousand pounds."

"Two thousand," Walter said, his vocal converter misinterpreting a private thought for an intended vocalization. Suddenly, he was glad he wasn't pink-skinned enough to blush.

"At least you're honest," said yet another chimp, smirking.

"Yeah, you're fat, and I've got an exclamation point in my name!" Pow! said, proudly. Walter ignored the declaration; he'd heard it many times before.

Zapp eyeballed Pow!, then continued. "Maybe if you weren't so fat, you could do *this*." The chimp stared at a pendant dangling from one of the chimp's matching necklaces—Walter had never been given a necklace. Suddenly, it started to quake.

"Isn't that cool?" said the chimp.

"Yeah," Walter had to admit. "It is."

A gloating voice: "Dr. Ron says we'll be able to move things with our minds in a year."

"When are you going to move things with your mind, Walter?" asked Pow!.

"Never! He's too fat!" Zapp said, and then there was laughter all around. Walter wanted to melt into the floor.

"Come on, lay off him a bit, will ya, guys?" said Ray, the smallest and weakest chimp.

Dark and burly Cosmo—Zapp's top enforcer—turned to Ray. "Yeah, just who do you think you are?"

Ray glared. "Sure, he's a fat-ass, but do you have to remind him all the time?"

Cosmo pushed out his chest and moved towards Ray. "Zapp will do what he wants to do, when he wants to do it."

Walter was glad they'd turned their focus on Ray. Walter almost liked the chimp. *Almost.*

"Come on. I just—"

Cosmo spat at Ray. "You're the weak link and you know it!"

"But—"

"You don't even have a space name!"

"Ray is a space name!" He wrung his hands, seemed to think. "Like Ray *gun!*"

"More like *Ray, shut the fuck up!*" Cosmo shouted.

Suddenly, the door to the science gym swung open. Dr. Ron emerged, thick arms folded across an ample, well-muscled chest. Dark circles were under his eyes. He'd looked a little tired for the past week, yet maintained a dominant presence. "What's going on here?" he asked.

Cosmo took steps back. Zapp looked at the floor. "Nothing, Dr. Ron," Zapp said.

"Glad to hear that. Now stop lollygagging and get your asses in here!" He flexed his biceps, kissed one of them. "Time to get pumped!"

Silently, the chimps filed past the door. Zapp, however, turned to Ray. "Walrus-lover," he whispered. Then, to Walter, he added, "Fat ass."

The walrus pretended not to hear as he flopped in behind the rest.

IN THE SCIENCE GYM

The Science Gym was huge and sterile—everything slick and shiny. There were no smells, no sounds—just the clangs, pings and beeps of machinery and equipment. Standard free weights and running boards were present, but also whirring, box-like gadgets lined with switches and diodes. Their functions remained a mystery to Walter, though he'd been hooked to their ports a time or two.

Deeper in the room, chimps were already going at it, hoisting dumbbells or bench pressing free weights or peddling stationary bikes like seasoned pros. Walter hated them so much.

Then he noticed Dr. Stephanie, who'd just stepped out from a change room. She'd donned a tiny spandex number, breasts pert against the fabric. It wasn't trashy like stuff worn by movie-women who hung around street corners. It was just…interesting.

Approaching him, she said, "Are you ready for a workout, cutie?"

"Not really," he replied.

"You need a better attitude than that."

"Can't," he said. "Just don't like it."

"But it's paying off." She ran her hands down his flank. "You're getting stronger by the day, and you were strong even before you got here."

Walter savored her touch, even as he noticed Dr. Ron staring at the two of them. "I was?"

"Of course you were." She continued touching him, fingers lingering over certain indentations and spots. "And your skin feels so firm and healthy. I'd almost think blubber could turn to muscle."

"It can?"

She started to smile. "Maybe if you want it enough."

"I want it hard, Dr. Stephanie."

"Then wish for it hard."

Walter began to do so, his face reddening under the strain.

She laughed. "Not that hard, Walter. Save your energy for the treadmill."

He turned from her. Facial implants responded to signals in his brain that made him scowl at the machine.

"Three minutes. That's all I ask."

Realizing there was no escape, he mounted the thing. Now, it was time to belly flop, to make the squelchy sounds he hated, faster than he'd ever imagined making them, again and again and again.

Dr. Stephanie switched on the treadmill, forcing the walrus into sudden and awkward motion. "You're doing great, Walter," she said. "Just great."

But Walter knew she was humoring him. He wasn't doing great, even with the treadmill on its lowest setting. He looked like an idiot, felt like one, too, and he couldn't turn away from the chimps—lifting, pressing, bending and stretching with total confidence—so he closed his eyes and imagined he was in a dark cave where only bats saw him flail.

On the other side of the room, Dr. Ron studied Walter while pretending to read from a clipboard. A minute passed. Lowering the clipboard, he began to slowly approach Dr. Stephanie. Once beside her, he said, "Walter's not doing so hot, is he?"

Walter was pulled from his cave as Dr. Stephanie replied, "Comparatively, maybe not, but he's making definite progress."

Dr. Ron prodded the walrus with a pen, added, "He's just not going fast enough."

"Well, he wasn't designed to run like a chimp."

Walter hated the sound of that word coming from Dr. Stephanie's mouth even more than the feel of the pen against his hide.

"Stand back," Dr. Ron said. "Let me try something."

"But your chimps..."

He looked over at them, raised a thumb. "Don't worry. They're doing fine on their own."

"Really, I think—"

Dr. Ron didn't let her finish. "We're dealing with a tub of blubber that needs to be turned into a man. Without extra *oomph*, you'll never get him past minimum guidelines, and I have seniority. No offense."

She smiled thinly. "None taken. Continue, please."

Dr. Ron leaned in so close that Walter smelled what he'd eaten for breakfast. Sardines, it seemed. The walrus felt suddenly hungry, but the sensation was blasted away when Dr. Ron shouted into his earflaps, "Run, Walter! Run! Space pirates are on your ass!"

Suddenly, in his mind, Walter saw these pirates—hideous, multi-tentacled man-things clutching scabbards with hands like claws.

He flopped faster, harder, in an attempt to escape them. His belly started to ache.

Dr. Stephanie placed a hand on Dr. Ron's shoulder. "Are you sure this is the best approach?"

"Does he have heart problems?"

"No."

"Then he'll be fine. Trust me." He turned back to Walter, screamed, "Keep running, you son of a bitch! Keep running!" It looked as though a blood vessel might explode in Dr. Ron's forehead. A bead of sweat rolled into his left eyeball. He didn't flinch.

Walter had no choice but obey. The space pirates were so close he could feel their hot, fetid breath steaming up his hide. In his chest, Walter's heart did a drum-solo. His lungs belonged to a dying ant.

Dr. Ron's mouth became an O. He smacked hands against the sides of his face. "Oh no, they got you! They got you and ripped you open, harpooned your blubber and rendered it to make oil for their lamps!"

Walter continued to flop, even as he felt guts being wrenched from his body, now just a fat, ugly and useless shell—but perhaps it had always been that way.

"Okay, you can stop now," Dr. Ron said, after another minute had passed. "You're dead."

Walter didn't question this. It seemed reasonable enough as he sagged down and the treadmill spilled him out onto the floor.

"Wow," Dr. Stephanie said. "Just wow."

Dr. Ron grinned. "He went faster than ever, right?"

"I guess he did, but I've never seen you do anything remotely similar with the chimps."

"Rest assured, I have. I just changed around the imagery for Walter."

"But—"

"No buts. I recommend you take a similar approach from now on. If you do, maybe he'll get someplace that matters."

"I'll consider it," Dr. Stephanie said, flatly. Then she turned from Dr. Ron and glanced down at Walter, who remained on the floor in a daze, staring up at the lights without blinking.

A HATEFUL WALRUS

On the return to Walter's room, Dr. Stephanie took the long way around with him, past unfamiliar halls, some of which he'd never before seen.

Walter wanted to speak, but spent a period in silence, considering his words deeply. Finally, he posed the question he needed to ask: "Are you considering it, Dr. Stephanie?"

She looked confused. "Considering what?"

"Doing things the way Dr. Ron does them."

"Of course not."

"Good," said Walter.

"Dr. Ron can be a bit of an old toughie, can't he?" Dr. Stephanie smiled. "He means well, though."

Walter was incredulous. "Does he?"

"Of course. Dr. Ron loves animals."

"I think he only loves chimps."

"Nonsense."

"He called me a son of a bitch, Dr. Stephanie."

"True." She paused, seemed to think. "But you've got to admit he made you run in a way I didn't think possible."

"Space pirates are scary."

"They're not that scary, Walter."

"Oh yes, they are."

Dr. Stephanie sighed, stopped walking. Her eyes met his in a way that made him want to flinch. "Aren't you in the least bit proud of yourself?"

He shook his head. "Dr. Ron makes me feel ashamed."

"He's a very accomplished man. His work with the chimps is—"

"I hate the chimps, Dr. Stephanie."

"It's wrong to hate anything."

"But they say such mean things to me. They tell me I'm fat."

"Well, they shouldn't do it, but if you hate something long enough, you'll become a hateful walrus, and who'd want that?"

"I can't help it!"

"You can help *anything*," Dr. Stephanie said. "You've just got to focus your mind."

At that moment, Walter felt like scraping his tusks against the wall. It was a common reaction to stress and frustration. "Can we talk about something other than Dr. Ron or the chimps?" he said.

"Okay then, what do you want to talk about?"

Walter didn't know. He wanted to ask her a lot of things—about her, about himself—but felt tongue-tied. At that moment, he heard something like a bark coming from a closed-off room to his right.

"What was that?" he asked.

"Not sure. Probably a dog."

Walter thought of Lassie and Rin Tin Tin. "I didn't know dogs were up here."

"There're a bunch of animals you've never seen."

"Are they going on space walks, too?"

"I'd say not."

"That's sad—so close to space, but they won't ever get to touch it."

When she laughed at this, he asked, "What's so funny, Dr. Stephanie?"

"Most of them don't even know of space, Walter."

He was boggled. He wanted to say, "How is that possible? To be so close, yet have no interest?" Instead, his converter said, "Possible, why? So close. No interest."

Dr. Stephanie got the gist. "It's that they aren't capable of having that interest," she said.

"I don't understand."

"Most animals aren't as smart as you or the chimps. They can't talk or think like you can."

"They can't?"

"You didn't entertain a human-level thought until you were seven years old, but you've made such great progress since then. Four or five years from now, you might have the equivalent of a college degree."

"But I could never be smarter than you, Dr. Stephanie. Are you the smartest woman who's ever lived?"

Again, she laughed a little. "There's nothing special about me. I'm not a genius, Walter. I just had a passion and did everything I could to see it realized."

"Wrong, Dr. Stephanie. You are very special."

She shrugged. "I don't feel special, just lucky to be up here with you—and all the others, too."

"What others?"

"There are pods upon pods in this station."

"And more doctors?"

"Of course."

"Have you seen them?"

"Some of them."

"How come *I've* never seen them?"

"Because they're in entirely different sectors. Really, Walter, I've never seen most of them myself. The few I have are doing similar research."

"With walruses?"

"No, you're the only walrus here."

"Oh." After a few moments of silence: "Will I at least be able to go to another pod; talk with the animals?"

"No. Only doctors and workers do that."

"What if I became a worker?" His face seemed to light up. "Or even a doctor?"

"I'm sorry, Walter. But you're a subject."

His face fell. He stopped walking.

Dr. Stephanie stopped, too. "Maybe I shouldn't have put it that way."

He looked up at her, expression plaintiff. "So, how long will I be a subject?"

"Well, always. But it's not a bad thing. I'd have nothing to do around here if not for you." She smiled. "You're the best subject of them all."

"I wish I could be something else."

She stroked his head. "Don't be glum. You're here, and so many things are going on, more things than you'll ever know."

"What do you mean?"

"For example, this is just a third of Pod Ten."

"Really? Wow."

"And there are twenty-three pods besides this one." She paused. "Would you like to see the outside of one of them?"

Walter did, more than anything, and extra time spent with Dr. Stephanie was all he needed to get back into the right frame of mind.

"Then follow me to my office."

Eagerly, he hobbled behind her.

BIG DOUGHNUT

After moving her desk from the wall so Walter could flop to it, Dr. Stephanie pulled back a curtain. It was like she was unveiling a gift to him. Walter looked out over that part of the station, the whole of which, he imagined, was shaped like a big doughnut. "So," he asked, "what do they do there?"

"Lots of unprecedented research."

He imagined jet packs and strobe lights and robots that could think, if not love, all existing so close, yet separated internally by locked pod doors and externally by space itself.

Dr. Stephanie continued. "Some of the stuff other pods are doing—well, it's just amazing. There're so many real-world applications, Walter. Believe me."

"Tell me more, Dr. Stephanie."

She paused. "I signed a waiver, said I'd say nothing to no one, but you're not a person, are you?"

"No," he said. "I'm a walrus."

"Okay, then. In one of the pods, they're inventing synthetic foodstuff designed to replace meat. Cattle will eat it, freeing grain for human consumption. Just think of the possibilities. World hunger could become a thing of the past."

Walter felt spellbound. His brain flashed to a phrase he'd heard in a movie. It seemed quite fitting.

"It's a miracle of modern science," he said.

Dr. Stephanie laughed. Walter saw her happy reflection behind his own in the window. He wished she'd put her arms around him, but she didn't.

NO BATH TODAY

On the way back, they passed the shower room. Dr. Stephanie didn't slow down, or even take a backwards glance. Walter, however, did.

"I thought you were going to bathe me," he said.

"Oh Walter, I'm so sorry. I forgot."

"There's still time."

"But I can't. We spent so long looking at that other pod, and I'm tired. It's been a long day."

"But you promised."

"I did, but it wasn't a big promise, Walter. It was just a small one."

"A promise is a promise, Dr. Stephanie, and I need to be clean."

She looked him over. "You're not dirty. A bath can wait."

The walrus grumbled.

"Come on. I showed you another pod, didn't I?"

"Yes, Dr. Stephanie. You did."

ICE STATION ZEBRA

Walter was sick of moping in his room. He felt like it was time for a movie.

At first, the walrus hadn't liked them. Other things in the room had seemed more interesting than whatever flickered on the boxy TV, and then he still thought of mussels more often than space. But, what seemed like a lifetime ago, he began to make sense out of the on-screen images and the patterns they created, ultimately finding amusement, horror, or arousal therein.

Horror movies were some of his favorites, though Dr. Stephanie didn't let him watch them very often. She preferred that he watch comedies. Once, she had directed him to some nature videos. He'd tried to watch one. Never again. If a new title sounded even remotely like that of a nature video, he removed it from the queue.

Initially, the documentary he'd watched had seemed kind of sexy, as the focus was on female walruses in heat. Walter watched with rapt attention. He could almost smell the spice of their exuded pheromones.

Then the killing started. Bull walruses didn't say anything before tearing into one another. There was no love in their eyes. No trace of compassion or understanding, no empathy—just rage and hatred and envy. And there was so much blood.

When all was said and done, the victim didn't move. His hide was a map of crisscrossing cuts, a massive gash on his flank. His body didn't ripple with the intake of breath.

Walter imagined the walrus' funeral, family members sobbing over the poor dead thing in its casket, soft music piped into the room from speakers above. The victor, however, just flopped away, back to his harem as though the corpse did not lie there, trickling blood.

Ultimately, Walter himself began to feel dominated. He wanted to drop his head, hide his tusks and cower low, to appear as a rock. And the movie's effect lingered long after he stopped watching it. Sometimes, he wondered if a big walrus might jump in front of him, cutting off his passage while alone after-hours in the mostly dark halls. It was silly, of course. He was the only physical walrus he'd seen, the others thousands of miles below him on Earth. But understanding that the fear was irrational did nothing to prevent it.

Walter wished there were other nature videos, ones that showed the loving, scholarly and articulate side of walrus life. He also wished more walrus-centric cinema was available in general. He'd only seen walruses in two of those, and they weren't the stars. In fact, they weren't even the supporting cast, just background zoo characters in one and barely seen arctic blobs in the other.

Walter decided he'd try to find a good walrus movie now. Scrolling through files, he ultimately chose *Icestation Zebra*. It sounded like something that might feature a walrus or two, though he was confused why a zebra might be in so cold a place.

He started the movie with the touch of an electro-finger against a screen. He returned to bed, started watching, but there were no zebras to be seen, and no walruses, either. It was just a mishmash of spy-related stuff that Walter barely understood.

Still, the flick was distracting enough to keep his mind active and slothful thoughts at bay, so he sat through the remainder of it. When the credits rolled, he considered selecting another, but realized it was past time for bed.

SLEEPLESS INHUMAN

Walter couldn't sleep, though he was eager to dream. Still, a dream alone would hardly suffice. He simply couldn't stop thinking about the thing Dr. Ron had done in the science gym, about the chimps and their ways.

Never before had he felt so tossed about by circumstance, so under the thumb of cruel, if not outright malevolent forces. Things were amassing against him, and there was no outside anchor to which he might cling.

He needed to find satisfaction in himself. He needed to act instead of being acted upon. No longer could he sit and take what he'd been given. It was an insult to his walrus-hood, and he had to treat it as such. He couldn't prove the chimps right; he couldn't be a wimp.

And if that meant hurting a few feelings, if not other living things, then so be it.

Walter arose from bed. He felt more resolute than ever. The chimps would get what was coming to them, oh yes.

THE STRING

The hall was dark and quiet. Sometimes, it could seem forbidding when Walter was the only thing there, but not now. The silence seemed like a conspirator, in on the plan with him.

He quieted his flops as he neared the door to the chimps' room. Once directly across from it, the walrus turned sideways and stared. Their door was identical to any other on this side of the station, flush against the facing on all sides, no way to pry it up. Maybe he could make use of his bulk, ram himself against the door until it gave in ... and then the chimps would feel the sheer power of his tusks.

But that was too brutal. He wasn't a brutal walrus, just pissed off.

Walter thought for a bit. The chimps had to have stuff sitting in cabinets or refrigerators. He could go into the laboratory, find something to make them sick—just nothing with a skull-and-crossbones label—and put it in their food.

Too bad he knew little about chemistry apart from the fact arsenic killed, which he learned from watching *Arsenic and Old Lace*. Strychnine killed, too, but he couldn't remember the title of the movie it was from, only that the film had been scary.

But no, that was going too far, too. He couldn't kill them, couldn't even hurt them, at least not too badly. He had to take hold of his anger, had to think, compose himself.

Walter felt stymied. With nothing practical to ponder, he began to wonder what their room was like. He doubted it was the same size as his own, not with all the chimps that had to live and sleep there. Did it have multiple compartments, or even whole different rooms? Was their bath shared, or did those bastards have private ones apiece?

And what sort of weird technology was hidden in there? Did their remote control float to them when they willed it to? Did they watch movies on holographic screens?

It was apparent: he couldn't do anything to the chimps.

Suddenly, he remembered college guys playing pranks on other college guys in a movie. A fire alarm sounded. The other college guys flopped out of their rooms much like walruses, only in t-shirts and underwear. It was a strange scene. Nevertheless, it had given him the best idea of the night. He could tie string across their door.

Walter imagined Zapp walking out first and tripping. He'd get a face full of floor. Might even break his legs. No epic space walk then, and Walter doubted Dr. Ron would let the others go without their precious leader.

He returned to his room, dug through his desk and ruffled through his things until he found a length of string.

Back at the chimps' door, Walter realized what should have been apparent earlier, that there was no way to tie the string because everything—doors, walls and ceilings—was on the same surface level, and there were no facings.

He hadn't thought things through. He grunted, disappointed that his once-brilliant plan had been thwarted by a lack of foresight.

Then it came to him.

Returning again to his room, he found some glue that Dr. Stephanie had given him for earlier art projects that proved, once and for all, that he was no artist. Walter had gotten the glue on his flippers and they stuck together until—in a panic— he found Dr. Stephanie, who applied a solvent. She'd said that she was disappointed in him; she thought he was mature enough to handle glue. She'd taken it away from him then and only returned it six months later.

The important thing, however, was that he had the glue now.

Walter squirted it on one side, near the bottom of the door. Then he squirted it on the other side. Holding the string out, he placed it into both dollops of glue. He only had to hold the ends for a few seconds before the string held fast.

Standing back, Walter surveyed his work.

Perfect.

A CHANGE OF HEART

Walter sat in his bed, no TV, no music. He stared up at the reflection of his nightlight on the metal ceiling.

It grated on him, the thought of the chimps falling over and hurting themselves. With the slight exception of Ray, they'd been nothing but total assholes to him, but never once had they hurt him physically.

And what if their bones got broken, or skin split? Would that give them free reign to declare the opening of Walrus Season?

The string had to go.

LIKE DEFEAT

The hall seemed foreboding again. Walter thought he heard something coming from behind a closed door. He put his ear to it, heard some bleeps.

That, he imagined, had to be the entry to one of the other sectors. No broom closet or shared bathroom would sound like that.

He moved to another door. There was only silence behind it. He was curious—and a little scared—and a part of him wanted to listen through others—but his primary focus was on removing the string from the chimps' door.

At the door, Walter stopped, looked down and regarded the string.

With a sigh, he broke it in the middle, tried to yank the string free from the glue, but couldn't. The act felt somewhat like defeat.

AN EVER-ENLARGING STAR

Orange fire and billows of gray smoke erupted from Space Walrus' backside as he soared across the galaxy in hyper-drive. The enemy ship, now tens of thousands of earth miles away, would soon be within sight. Locking down its coordinates hadn't posed a problem. Space Walrus' mind was attuned to even the most obscure fiber of the universal matrix.

He contemplated his past as he flew. Such meditations were common, but haunting. His earliest years were lost years, and his mother and father less than shadows to him. It sometimes seemed to Space Walrus that he'd always existed, that time begat itself upon his formation. Still, he knew two special walruses had been his parents.

Long ago, an old oracle had told him that each mission the walrus undertook reflected a unique, individual aspect of his past and that feats of heroism would someday culminate in revelation. Space Walrus didn't know if he believed this, or even if it mattered whether or not the hole was filled. Maybe he would have grown fat and complacent if not for the nagging sense of loss.

Up ahead, Space Walrus noticed what appeared to be an ever-enlarging star, but understood it was the enemy ship, taking shape.

Ovular and obsidian, it bristled with harsh angles and serpentine protuberances that unfurled in hooks and spirals. Other parts waved like tentacles.

Space Walrus de-activated his hyper-drive function. Smoke and flame disappeared from his backside as he stopped within mere inches of the ship

The hero felt ill, just being in the ship's presence. Never before had he encountered one with an aura. It was dark, foreboding and felt masculine. Space Walrus wondered if the ship itself was a living entity.

Shoving odd questions aside, he surveyed the exterior. It seemed impregnable, but there had to be an opening. He felt around smooth surfaces for a hatch. If only he could catch a grip.

Finally, he caught one.

Space Walrus slid the edges of his flippers inside the narrow space between the secreted hatch and the body of the ship. With brute force, he pried away metal and slipped through the breach to a long tube that led to an airlock. When it opened, he entered a hall that resembled a fetid, dripping wet cave. Fat tufts of bioluminescent mold grew wild. It was the only light source, but the light it produced was an illuminating black.

The atmosphere around him: deep red, scarlet even. Clearly, the things here didn't breathe oxygen, but that was of no concern to Space Walrus. He could take anything into his lungs, or nothing at all.

His footsteps echoed hollow. It seemed he was alone.

Space Walrus thought he smelled meat.

Suddenly, space beasts poured out from every door into the hall, horrible things—rhinoceroses with snakes for limbs and mutated polar bear-vultures with worms like male genitalia slipping in and out of gaping eye sockets. All were bent on the destruction of truth and love and beauty. All clutched guns in their many hands.

Space Walrus' eyes and tusks started to gleam with inner light. If, to ensure Princess Stephanie's safety, he had to tear off ten thousand space beast heads, bathe in their blood until he all but drowned, then so be it.

But the beasts fired their guns.

The weapons were loaded with bullets laced with Karmahexadrine 5, the only compound in the universe that could harm him, rob him of his powers and leave him nothing more than a pile of quivering blubber.

Space Walrus tried to reach out, find light, but there was none. The world darkened beyond black, then darkened still.

AN UNEXPECTED PHONE CALL

Something rang out. Walter awoke with a start, thinking it might be a disintegrating ray, zipping towards him. Then he realized it was only the phone in his room.

Walter flopped groggily to the receiver. Robo-hands picked it up. "Hello," he said.

"Howdy, fuck breath," said a slurred, sloshy voice.

"Dr. Ron?"

"You bet your fat ass this is Dr. fucking Ron."

The man sounded similar to stumbling, ruddy-faced people he'd seen in movies, people that needed help into cars destined to plow over a pedestrian or two. "Are you drinking, Dr. Ron?"

"Of course I'm drinking! The ship came in last week, hallelujah!" Then his voice was a low growl. "But don't say a word about this to Dr. Stephanie, you hear? She doesn't know."

"Yes, I—"

A sudden roar: "*Yes?* As in, *yes, you'll tell her!*"

"No! I'll never say a word!"

For almost a minute, Walter heard only the sounds of Dr. Ron taking big, strong gulps. Finally, after a belch, "So, what have you been up to?"

"Well, I—"

"You were masturbating earlier, weren't you?"

Aghast, Walter said nothing

The voice was more insistent. "Weren't you?"

"Yes! Yes, I was!"

A chuckle. "Dr. Stephanie knows, too. She records every *incident* in a little black book."

Walter wanted to die.

"Dr. Stephanie may be asleep now, but I'm watching you." A pause. "I always watch. I watch the empty halls on monitors in my room, night after night. Sometimes it takes hours for my eyes to close; sometimes they never close. I see so much—more than you'll ever know."

"Okay, but it's late and I—"

"Don't think it's easy, Walter, being able to see so many things. It's hard. So very hard. I—I feel so twitchy sometimes, like every part of my body is aflame, but there's never a rash."

"I don't know if I can help you with that, Dr. Ron."

"And my heart, it just pounds away. Like it's going to beat right out of my chest and out my fucking throat!"

"I'm—I'm sorry you're having this problem, Dr. Ron. I—"

"And my hair, it's oily. Always oily no matter what I do. I just can't get my hair clean up here! It's impossible. It cannot happen. There's no way. No way whatsoever, Walter."

"Maybe, uh—try new...shampoo."

Dr. Ron kept rambling: "God knows I want it to be different, but it's not. I've even blacked out a few times. Whenever I wake up, I think I'm back on Earth, and I feel so good, Walter, so very good, like I'm a kid again. Then I look out my window, see the black pit of space yawning wide, and want to claw my fucking eyes out. Claw them out and eat them, so I never have to see it again!"

"That's terrible. I—"

"And, just yesterday, thinking about eating my eyes made me realize I hadn't eaten in two days. And all I could think was, *gee, has it been that long?* But all food sours my gut these days! It makes me puke! It turns my shit green and purple and blue!"

Walter's stomach flipped. "Are you sure you should be telling me this?"

"It doesn't matter what I tell you, Walter. Nothing matters anymore. It's never mattered, and never will."

"I'm sorry you feel this way."

He snorted. *"You're sorry I feel this way?"*

"Yes, yes! I am! Very, very sorry!"

"Walter, you're the reason this is happening to me. You and you alone!"

"But—"

"Shut up! I fucking hate your retarded voice!"

He thought, *then give me an upgrade.* His converter spoke the words aloud.

Dr. Ron's tone turned condescending. "An uppity little bitch, aren't you?"

Backtracking, Walter realized, was impossible. "The chimps got theirs, and—"

"You, Walter, can go fuck yourself."

He was taken aback. Before, he'd only heard the f-word in movies.

"Go fuck yourself," Dr. Ron pressed. "I mean it literally."

"What?"

"I want to hear you do it, right now."

"You mean—"

"Yes! Do it!"

Walter wondered how he might simulate the act so it sounded convincing over the phone.

"Do it, Walter! Do it now!"

He had no time to think. He rubbed the phone against his body, tried to grunt through his converter. He'd never felt more awkward in his life.

"Is this good enough?" he asked.

"No! Harder! Faster!"

Walter did so, to the best of his ability.

"Now splooge!"

Via the converter, intended spurting-noises sounded like faint blips of static. Still, Dr. Ron was pleased. "Good, Walter. Good," he said. "That's exactly what I wanted to hear."

"Oh, okay. Uh—"

"Goodnight, Walter. I'll be seeing you."

"Dr. Ron?" Walter said, but the other end had already gone dead.

The walrus trembled as he laid down the receiver.

NEEDING DR. STEPHANIE

Walter couldn't get back to sleep after Dr. Ron's call. He felt even guiltier about the string, and there was a sick feeling in his gut, knowing that Dr. Ron was probably watching him at that moment. If only Dr. Stephanie were to come to him, stroke his head and say soothing words, then true rest might be obtainable.

No longer could he sit in stasis. He had to contact her, something Walter had only dared to do twice before. But Dr. Stephanie probably wasn't even asleep yet. Surely, there was no harm in calling her.

He got out of bed, picked up the phone, dialed 8, the number of Dr. Stephanie, and waited.

He was nervous.

"Hi, Dr. Stephanie," he said, when the other lines opened.

She sounded surprised to hear his voice. "Oh hello, Walter! To what do I owe this pleasure?"

It took him a few moments to build up the courage to make his request. "I want you to— I mean, can you come to my room, talk with me?"

"I'm so busy right now."

That was the last thing he wanted her to say. "But will you please, Dr. Stephanie? Pretty please? I really need it."

She laughed. "With sugar on top?"

"With sugar on top, if it'll make you come."

"You don't have to make me come, Walter."

"I don't?"

"No. I'll be right over."

WHO MADE ME SPECIAL?

Dr. Stephanie entered Walter's room, sat down.

"It's rare that you call me, Walter." She looked him over quickly. "Everything okay?"

"I'm fine, Dr. Stephanie. I just wanted to talk with you."

"About what?"

He wished he had feet to shuffle. "Well, I don't know…"

She sidled up closer to him. "It seems like there's something you've wanted to talk to me about for some time, but you've never gotten around to doing it."

After a little consideration: "I want to know more about what things were like before I got here."

"You know I can't tell you that."

"Just a little bit, please."

"Dr. Ron doesn't tell the chimps, yet, back on Earth, one of them did something truly amazing."

Walter felt pangs of jealousy. "Was it Zapp? What did he do that was so special?"

"Well, if he can't tell the chimp, then I can't tell you. Makes sense, doesn't it?"

He frowned, but nodded. "I guess so."

"And aren't things a little more exciting with a touch of mystery?"

"More frustrating, you mean."

She smiled. "Just trust me when I say you're a very special walrus."

Walter was confused. "Who made me special?"

"Well, we did."

His eyes widened. He looked around the room, searching

49

for hidden cameras. "We're the only ones here!"

"I mean my team, of course. I was just one of twelve on it. And it wasn't like I did everything myself; I just helped in my own small way to make you what you are, and I'm helping you now."

"But you know so much about me. Shouldn't I know a little of it, too?"

"I'm not sure—"

"Just a little bit, Dr. Stephanie," he implored.

Following a moment of silence: "Maybe you deserve to know."

"Yes, Dr. Stephanie. I do. Tell me."

"Okay, Walter. But say nothing of this to Dr. Ron, okay?"

"Don't worry," he said. "I won't."

She began her story. The walrus soaked in her words.

DR. STEPHANIE'S STORY

"The government did something stupid. Let's say that. And it polluted a large swath of the arctic in a way that... Well..."

Walter had never seen Dr. Stephanie tongue-tied. This worried him.

"The damage was unspeakable, terrible beyond words. The single most horrific environmental disaster to occur, ever—and nobody thinks about it!"

To Walter, it sounded like the stuff of nightmares. "Why?" he asked.

"Because human population centers weren't affected! If it's a bunch of animals and pristine arctic land, then who the hell cares, right?"

Walter wasn't accustomed to hearing Dr. Stephanie use such words, or that tone of voice.

"And the bastards tried to cover it up, deny it ever happened. It would have been easy for them to do it, too—if a video hadn't been posted online. Most thought it was fake at first, some expensive Hollywood trick, but it wasn't.

"Animals had changed, the landscape, too. Holes in the ground opened up and moved like mouths. The worst of them had rocks for teeth. Just imagine what would have happened had it spilled in a city!"

In Walter's head, it looked like a mix of all the horror movies he remembered seeing. His tusks felt very small. "That's really scary, Dr. Stephanie," he said.

She broke eye contact. "Maybe I've said too much."

"No, don't stop!"

"Are you sure you want to hear more?"

He nodded.

"It might get even scarier..."

"But I've got to know, Dr. Stephanie."

She continued:

"The mutated walruses were the most fearsome. They killed on sight. Anything non-mutated was fair game. The closest I can come to describing them is a walrus/jellyfish hybrid, with fangs.

"What's worse, the mutated walruses had *powers*. They were able to project their conscious will at those who pursued them, get in their minds and scare them so bad that no one thought of approaching. Naturalists had never encountered such animals; they didn't know how to deal with them."

"Did they find a way?" Walter asked.

"Yes. Helmets finally worked, and—if you'd believe it— they were made of tin-foil.

"So they put on their tin-foil hats, got past the first onslaught with minds intact, but the same couldn't be said about bodies. Eleven men went out that day; three returned to base camp alive."

"How could so few walruses take so many men?"

"They overran then. Mutated walruses started dividing asexually, splitting to become thousands of abominations that would become millions, if something hadn't been done. Eventually, it was decided to nuke the area.

"No one will eat fish out of nearby waters for many, many years. People will be able to live on the surrounding land at some point, but only after we're dead."

Walter felt dazed by her story. "What does all that have to do with me?" he asked.

"You lived through it, Walter."

He was baffled. "I did?"

"Yes. They found you cowering under a rock. You were the only surviving, non-mutated walrus in a hundred and sixty mile radius. That's why you were chosen to come up here with me; it was America's way of atoning."

COLD AND ALONE

Dr. Stephanie sat with Walter long after she'd finished her tale. In his mind, he saw red, snot-coated eyes. Snarling lips and gaping mouths. Tusks that never ended and looked like so many knives. "I remember monsters," he said. "And I remember the rock, the bad place. I thought it was a dream I had when I was a pup."

Dr. Stephanie sighed. "Maybe it should have always seemed that way."

It was all coming back to him now.

"And I was so cold, so alone."

"I know, Walter," Dr. Stephanie soothed. "But you weren't totally alone. A polar bear hiding in a cave less than a half kilometer from you survived, but you never got to meet him."

"There's Space Polar Bear?"

"Oh no," she said. "That would be a terrible idea."

"So, are any, uh, mutant walruses still around?"

"They've been gone a long time. You'll never have to deal with them again."

"Are you sure?"

"Very sure."

STRAPPED TO A GURNEY

Space Walrus came to and saw that he was strapped to a gurney.

Hideous space beasts glared down at him. One, dressed in a smock, removed surgical instruments from a folded cloth and arranged them on a table. The beast studied the selection, letting a gnarled hand glide over the lot. Finally, it chose a multi-pronged device that seemed part melon scoop, part bone saw.

The beasts, he realized, were vivisectionists. They intended to harvest his parts, like the Inuit had with his Earth-bound cousins, perhaps for some strange fuel, or merely for fun.

The Head Vivisector gestured to an anesthesiologist-beast. It reached for a mask, connected via tube to a black machine, and strapped it over Space Walrus' face. He heard a sound like a snake's hiss once the anesthesiologist opened a valve.

But the joke was on them all. The hero could hold his breath forever, and the effects of the Karmahexadrine-5 laced bullet were fading.

He strained to lift his flippers from his sides. Straps deformed with tension. They'd reach their breaking point soon. Space Walrus would then show these beasts what it meant to hurt.

He thrashed his tail. "Just give me a second," he said, a kill-gleam glistening in his eyes.

A second later, the lowermost strap broke.

Space Walrus' swooping tail slashed a space beast assistant, cleaving it in half.

Another escaped, but with a severed hand.

As others endeavored to secure Space Walrus' lower half, the Head Vivisector rammed a syringe into the walrus' flank.

It smiled loathsomely as the green and syrupy payload was delivered.

Instantly, Space Walrus' whipping tail became a flaccid thing, capable of harming no one. "You won't stop me with—" he tried to say. "You can't—and I am...you.. I..."

Words tumbled in his brain. His mouth felt like a stranger's mouth, his eyelids like lead curtains. An inner voice told him, *don't think; just sleep.*

In his final cognizant moment—as the Head Vivisector twisted a knob on his surgical implement, revealing additional hooks and barbs and blades—Space Walrus considered his failure. Princess Stephanie would never be saved. Her blood would cover him for the short time he seemed destined to remain alive.

THE NEXT DAY

Walter woke up.

Yet another exercise session was scheduled in a few hours. He dreaded encountering Dr. Ron. Would he even be there? Maybe he'd drunk himself sick the night before. Perhaps he was still puking into his Space Commode.

The walrus could only hope.

Walter pulled on his sweatband and slipped out the door. He hadn't gone far when he heard footsteps. Heavy Dr. Ron footsteps.

He looked around, though he knew there was no place to hide.

The man turned a corner into view and approached him. Walter froze in his spot. He didn't blink. Somehow, he managed to eek out, "You... You—No... I... Dr. Stephanie, help!"

"Excuse me?" said Dr. Ron, ever nearer.

He regained control of his converter. "Don't fuck me up, Dr. Ron!"

Stopping before Walter: "Where did you hear that kind of language?"

"From you! The phone call last—"

Dr. Ron stopped him. "What phone call?"

"Last night!"

"I think you're having an episode. Why would I call you?"

"I don't know! You were drunk!"

"What are you talking about, Walter? I don't drink. Everyone knows that."

"But—"

His tone was sterner. "It must have been a dream."

"No, you were freaked out and—"

"I said it must have been a dream! I made no phone call!" He slammed his fist against the wall so hard Walter feared the station might leave orbit. "And I don't drink!"

"Okay! You made no phone call!"

He slammed the wall again. Veins throbbed. "And I don't drink!"

Suddenly, Walter wished that robo-arms were long enough to shield his eyes. "And you don't drink!"

"Good, Walter. Good." He shook an admonishing finger. "Glad you know your place."

He cringed. "I know my place."

"You're a walrus." Dr. Ron turned his finger like a killer might twist a knife lodged in someone's gut. "Don't get uppity!"

With that, Walter followed Dr. Ron into the science gym quietly, his head down. With relief, he noticed that Dr. Stephanie was already there.

But it seemed she was preparing to leave.

"Where are you going?" he asked, hoping she'd say "the other side of the room."

Rather, she said, "Sorry, Walter, but I just found out I have to go."

That meant no treadmill. No heart palpitations or labored breaths. Walter smiled inwardly.

"But don't worry," she continued. "Dr. Ron agreed to work with you today."

Relief segued into horror. "No! He can't! Don't leave me, Dr. Stephanie!"

"I must. I'm needed on the other side of the station."

"It can wait!"

"Dr. Ron is perfectly capable of taking care of you."

"Please, I—"

"Let her go, Walter," said Dr. Ron, matter-of-factly.

Walter turned quickly to Dr. Stephanie, presented her with the saddest, most desperate expression his implants could muster. "Do you have to?"

"Yes, Walter. But I'll make it up to you, I promise."

"If you promise..."

"I do." She waved then. "Bye, Walter. I'll see you soon."

The door closed. Alone with Dr. Ron, Walter felt prickly.

"Relax," the doctor said. "I only want to talk with you before we begin."

"You do?"

"Sure."

"And that's all?"

"For now, yes."

Walter didn't like the doctor's phrasing, but said, "Okay. We'll talk."

"Good." Dr. Ron patted himself. "Now take a seat on my lap."

"What!"

"Just kidding." He laughed, drew in a deep breath. "So tell me, what is it you want more than anything?"

"To go out in space, like the chimps."

"You want to go out in space? A big, flabby thing like yourself?" Dr. Ron locked his gaze on Walter. "You realize you're a walrus, right?"

"Of course I do."

"Well, a space walk isn't in the cards," he said. "Want to know why it's not?"

Walter said nothing, just looked at the door that led out into the hall, wishing he were somewhere—anywhere—behind it.

"Because you're fat and ugly! Just look at your body!"

"I don't have a mirror."

"Doesn't matter! You know what you look like! You know what Dr. Stephanie has to put up with!" Dr. Ron panned his hand across the room and pointed. "There, look at the chimps' bodies. Focus on Zapp's and Cosmo's especially."

Walter gave them a cursory glance; he didn't want to look at the chimps unless he had to.

"No, I mean *study them*," Dr. Ron pressed. "Do you see even an ounce of blubber?"

Walter shook his head.

The doctor smiled, but not like Dr. Stephanie. He nudged the walrus. "I bet you think Zapp is sexy."

"Uh, no. I—"

"That's because he is sexy, Walter." Dr. Ron turned to the chimp. "Zapp, pull down your shorts and pose for this tub of lard!"

"But, Dr. Ron—"

"Do it! Pose!"

Zapp resigned himself, lost his shorts with a high kick and began to pose and flex in his little blue briefs.

"Focus on that," Dr. Ron said, his voice slithering into Walter's ears. "Focus hard."

"I—I—I—"

"Are you focusing?"

"I'm focusing!" Walter said, though he wished desperately that he could stop.

"Now dance!" Dr. Ron screamed at the chimp. "Yeah, that's the stuff! Pretend that's a pole there, Zapp! Awesome!"

Walter felt sick. Still, he was amazed that the chimp was so limber.

After a minute of continued gyration, Dr. Ron shouted, "Pull up your shorts!" He turned to Walter, leered. "That was hot shit, wasn't it?"

"I, uh—I, uh—"

"Would you like to be hot shit, too?"

Walter, not sure whether or not he wanted to be hot shit, simply nodded.

"I said, do you want to be hot shit?"

"Yes, sir!" he said. "I'd very much like to be hot shit, sir!"

"Well, you must expect additional therapy if you hope to reach the next level, and the next, and the one after that..."

"Maybe I don't want—"

"No backtracking, Walter! I hate backtrackers! You've got to take all I can throw at you. Swallow it down and say, ummmm, may I have more!"

"I don't want to swallow—"

"Wrong!" He lowered his voice, gestured with a finger. "Come, join me by the computer."

Dr. Ron began walking. Walter stood there.

"Walter, get your blubbery ass over here now!"

"Yes! Yes, Dr. Ron!" Slowly—even more slowly than usual—he approached the doctor, who tapped his fingers against the computer as he waited.

"Took you long enough," Dr. Ron said when the walrus stopped a few feet from him.

"I can only go so fast."

"Of course, and that's part of the problem, isn't it?"

Walter said nothing to this. He glared at the computer untrustingly. "What does that do?" he asked.

"Oh, it just monitors bio-rhythms."

"I'm not sure I want my bio-rhythms monitored."

"Of course you do," Dr. Ron said, and turned on the machine. Walter took a flop backwards.

"There's no need to be scared."

Walter, however, felt there was plenty need to be scared.

Suddenly, Dr. Ron reached out and grabbed Walter's head, tugging on it to expose a port in his orange skullcap. Then he plugged a cable linked to the computer into it. "Don't worry," he said, "you won't feel a thing."

Dr. Ron was almost right. It didn't hurt. But it was weird. Too weird, even.

Suddenly, it seemed that he was free from his body, but, just as quickly, he felt as though he had linked with the ship on a mental level, then similarly with the walls and the floor and the equipment in the room. But Walter didn't want to be part of any of those things. He wanted to be a walrus.

Dr. Ron removed the cable from Walter's skull port. The world as he knew it returned immediately. "Okay," the doctor said, "your vitals indicate you can withstand a throttling."

Walter had regained his ability to think in words. "What?"

"A throttling, Walter."

"Oh god."

"I want you to know something: I'm not at all like Dr. Stephanie. I like my challenges direct and life-altering." He paused, smiled. "Are you ready to be completely and utterly altered, Walter?"

"I—uh—no. I—"

Dr. Ron pointed. "Then get over to that machine!"

Walter eyeballed it as he flopped behind Dr. Ron. It certainly wasn't a computer. He wasn't sure it was even exercise equipment. It looked more like evil stuff from science fiction movies he'd seen—big, black and looming.

Closer still, Walter noticed a white skull and crossbones, overlaid against a black background. Whether it was on a bottle or marking the location of treasure in a cave, it usually meant danger was near.

The walrus saw a warning label.

"It says—"

"I don't care what it says! It's time to do your crunches and scrunches!"

"I can't. I—"

"Get into the machine! I won't tell you again!"

Walter did as he was told. Dr. Ron began to strap him to a vertical gurney within the pod.

"Why so many straps?"

"Because this is going to shake your shit up good." Dr. Ron tightened another strap. "In a few seconds, you'll be grateful for them."

"I don't want my shit shaken!"

"No choice, Walter. If you want to be a space hero, you've got to have your shit shaken."

"No! Please, no!"

The doctor laughed. He turned from Walter. "Zapp, please mind the inductor and increase the voltage when I tell you to do so."

Walter thought it was against protocol to let an animal

guide another animal's training; *he'd* never been allowed to help. But Zapp put down the dumbbells, took his position. He looked gleeful.

"Crank it up," Dr. Ron said.

The pod door closed. With a rumble, the machine powered on. It wasn't so bad at first, just the gentle sensation of pressure on all sides, something Walter could get used to.

Suddenly, he heard Dr. Ron's voice, muted but understandable. "In seconds, you'll feel the equivalent of thirty-five Gs of force against your body. The average human can stand no more than eight Gs, but I think such a big ass walrus should be able to stand a lot more. And if you can stomach thirty-five, we might go up to fifty!"

He thrashed in the straps. "No! Not fifty, Dr. Ron!"

"Nonsense, Walter. This is a grand experiment. You'll be the first walrus to ever experience such *pressure*."

"Stop, please! You—"

At that moment, pressure increased ten-fold. Tighter and tighter, Walter had no idea how his parts were squeezing together so firmly without bones breaking. "Faster! Harder!" he shouted, his vocal converter substituting antonyms for the intended words.

"That's the spirit, Walter!" Dr. Ron gave the signal for Zapp to increase the voltage. "You'll be a peanut when I'm through with you!"

The pressure was unrelenting. Walter felt as though he were being compressed to the size of a tuna and then forced into a can.

"Can't...scrunch...anymore!" he wanted to shout.

"You can and you must! If you don't, you'll never do a space walk!"

But Walter didn't hear him. It felt like the world itself wanted to crush his body, reduce it to component parts, then further still to base elements, and then to nothing at all. He knew then that he was going to die, if he wasn't dead already.

Suddenly, pressure dropped. The pod door opened. Walter spilled out onto the floor.

Dr. Ron approached him. "That was a bit extreme, wasn't it?"

The walrus said nothing.

"Well, I can be an extreme kind of guy." He tapped his foot, waited a bit. "Come on. Get up." He nudged Walter's bulk with his shoe. "You're making me sick."

"Want to...stay on...floor...little longer."

The doctor stopped nudging him. "Whatever. Have your own way."

"Good. Body like...jelly."

"Of course it is. You don't want to know how many pounds of pressure you just withstood, Walter. Forty-two Gs! It blows my mind!"

"Glad not...fifty."

Dr. Ron got down on his hands and knees then, his face just inches from Walter's. "Want to know something?" he asked. "I arranged it so Dr. Stephanie had to leave today. I set her to work on a task, said it needed to be done right away, but that wasn't true." His smile showed Walter many teeth. "And you're not going to say a thing because you know what I'd do to your ass. Isn't that right?"

He nodded.

"Say it, Walter! Say it!"

"I know what you'd do to my ass!"

Dr. Ron clutched a roll of blubber near the walrus' backside. "You bet you know."

Walter had no idea, but was too terrified to admit it.

The doctor relinquished his hold, turned to walk away. "Have a nice day, Walter," he said.

"Yeah, have a nice day," mimed Zapp, who raised his middle finger and looked smugly over at the walrus until his trainer closed the door behind them.

Walter was still lying there when Dr. Stephanie poked her head into the gym. Over an hour had passed. "Dr. Ron said I might find you here," she said. "He told me you had a stellar workout today, that you're making great progress."

"He said that?"

"I just hope he didn't push you too hard."

This was Walter's chance to tell Dr. Stephanie about the phone call, the bad workout, but he remembered Dr. Ron's threat: *And you're not going to say a thing because you know what I'd do to your ass.*

"Dr. Ron…accomplished man," he muttered.

"Yes he is, Walter." Dr. Stephanie was smiling. "Now go to the shower room and get ready."

"Really? You mean it?"

"Of course. I made sure to finish my other work early just so I wouldn't miss your bath time."

Typically, he was bathed after workouts, but lately his schedule had not gone according to routine. He felt somewhat grateful that the evil machine had immobilized him. Otherwise, Dr. Stephanie might not have found him here.

"I'm going to stop by my office," she said. "I'll see you in the shower in thirty minutes." She left the gym.

At least ten minutes passed before Walter's body had composed itself enough to move. Even then, he felt like an accordion as he made his way to the shower room.

SPARKLES

Walter rocked back and forth inside the shower room just below the nozzle, bounded by raised concrete sides where water would soon collect and drain. Dr. Stephanie was due to arrive at any moment, and her hands would lather soap all over him, run water down his back, sponge and towel him off.

He would be clean again.

But still he waited, until it seemed that he'd waited ten minutes. Maybe he was just being impatient. Perhaps it had only been five, though it was rare that she kept him waiting even that long.

He was powerless to do anything but think about Dr. Stephanie and the bath and the nice conversation they'd surely have during it. He wished she would hurry. He wished his arms were as long and his hands as dexterous as hers. Then he could turn on the water himself, and maybe she would hear the water and come running.

Hours seemed to pass. Had she decided she was too busy again? Was Dr. Ron talking to her?

Yes. He was.

Walter jerked when the door opened. He heard footsteps and saw Dr. Stephanie enter the shower room, wearing one of the three two-piece bikinis she always wore when she bathed him. This time, she sported the silvery blue one. *Nice*, he thought. It flattered her and fit her perfectly, but the red one with sparkles was his favorite.

With her, she carried an orange plastic bucket; brush, soap and sponge inside it. Walter couldn't wait to feel the touch of all three against his hide.

"I thought you'd never come," Walter said.

"I'm sorry, but I got tied up."

He imagined Dr. Ron tying up Dr. Stephanie and grimaced.

"What's wrong, Walter?"

"Nothing," he said.

"You just made a funny face." She smiled down at him, shook the bucket. "So, are you ready for your bath?"

"I'm always ready, Dr. Stephanie."

She took a seat on a little wooden stool, placed the bucket beside her, removing the sponge first. When she bent over, Walter saw a hint of ass. He looked away quickly.

Dr. Stephanie sat up, frowned at him. "You look tense," she said.

"No," he replied, finally. "Just bummed out." Walter wished his vocal converter had said "tired" instead of "bummed out," but he'd watched *Fast Times at Ridgemont High* a few days beforehand. Spicolli's voice still echoed in his brain.

Dr. Stephanie hefted a thick, bristled brush and approached the walrus. "Well, this'll make you feel a whole lot better."

Walter knew that to be true.

AN AWKWARD BATH

Dr. Stephanie started with his back this time, directing the opening spray of the showerhead there. Then came the sponge. It felt like heaven, rubbing up and down his leathery hide. He leaned into her scrubbings, letting the bristles of her brush scratch all over him, no longer content to let the doctor be the only active party.

"You help me bathe you, Walter. I appreciate it."

"You appreciate me?"

"I appreciate all strong, capable animals. You're a strong, capable animal, aren't you?"

"Yes. Yes, I am."

Dr. Stephanie turned her attention to the bottom of his chin. After the last scrub, she caressed his face. Walter rubbed his whiskers against her arm.

"I'm a worthy animal, too."

"What?"

Words dissolved as she started to scrub just above his front left flipper. That was the spot. Walter's head tilted; his mouth hung slightly ajar, an unconscious reaction to pleasure directed to that area. Instantly, the training session seemed ages ago, and then like it'd never happened at all. Dross had been stripped away from his being, along with all his darker thoughts. Now, he felt nothing but the soft, pleasant and warm sensations of an almost-but-not-quite empty mind.

Dr. Stephanie's voice bubbled up, seemingly from the ether. "I love bathing you."

"I know," he said, and that was all he could say before fantasy again claimed him, and Space Walrus sat in a hot tub filled with the warm, blue juice of space grapes, the greatest of all cleansers. He was told to wait there, that his bathers had to get *limbered up* first. Space Walrus didn't know what this meant, but had liked the sound of it.

He would be growing anxious, provided the feel of the space grape juice around him—soaking into him—wasn't so *fine*. It felt like it was going deeper than the mere epidermis, deeper even than the dermis. Perhaps it was cleansing his very cells, from the inside out.

The door creaked open. Space Walrus turned his head in the direction of the sound. Eight women clad in silver, metallic bikinis had entered. The bottoms had hinged doors on them. Space Walrus wondered whether or not he would open those doors.

He would.

"Hello, ladies," he said.

They just giggled. They were servant girls. Perhaps they didn't understand his language, or any other one. Saying nothing, but without hesitation, they climbed into the bath. In seconds, he felt their hands all over him.

"Almost finished," Dr. Stephanie said.

The fantasy disintegrated; Walter wasn't ready to let it go. "Can you sponge me a little more? I still feel dirty."

"But you look clean."

"Please. Please, I'm so dirty."

She looked closer at him. "Sometimes it's not easy, getting inside all your cracks and crevasses." She scrubbed harder. "Your skin is like a map."

Walter's eyes rolled up in their sockets.

Space Walrus realized the women each had a third eye, invisible when closed, but now opening in their foreheads. Radiant golden light poured out, enrapturing him. One after the other, the strange and beautiful women straddled the walrus.

"Come on, Walter. Help me get you flipped over."

Walter came back to himself with a start. *Oh god, not now!*

Immediately, his voice converter turned that thought into words.

"What?" she said as she continued to turn him, and he continued to allow her to do so; Walter could never deny Dr. Stephanie.

Wait, please!, he wanted to say, but said nothing, the converter having now misread the intended vocalization as a mere thought.

The turning process complete, Walter tried to cover himself. Electro-arms weren't long enough to reach his junk. He closed his eyes. Dr. Stephanie failed to notice his horror.

"See, that wasn't so—oh my god, Walter!"

He sputtered. "I'm so...hot...I mean...embarrassed. I—I'm sorry. I don't—I wasn't. I—"

Her shocked expression faded. She moved quickly to stroke his head. "Don't worry, Walter. It's okay."

He pulled away from her touch. "No, it's not!"

"You're a male walrus. You have certain feelings. I understand. It's perfectly natural."

"Is it?"

"Of course it is." She grabbed the rag, moved it towards him, but looked down and said, "I'm going to wait until you stop bulging so much to clean you down there, okay?"

"Oh god."

She continued to regard his walrushood; Walter couldn't look her in the eyes. He imagined his size had shrunk to a new low. He already considered himself small, as other walruses on nature shows he'd watched—the evil walruses—had staggeringly huge phalluses that they used to plunge into screaming females.

After almost a minute of silence: "There, it seems to be going down fast. It's just a little thing now."

Walter cringed.

"Stop. Don't be embarrassed."

"I can't help it!"

Suddenly, Dr. Stephanie seemed almost coy. "So, what were you thinking about? An old girlfriend you had on the floe?"

Walter felt the need to retreat safely inside himself.

"I bet you were," she continued.

"I don't think I ever had a girlfriend. Don't think I ever made love. Think I'm...a virgin."

"I'm sure a walrus like you had lots of girlfriends."

"Don't know. Don't remember that time. Doesn't seem real."

She resumed scrubbing him. Though he felt her towel on his penis, he was too mortified at the thought of having another erection to achieve it.

"You know something? If you were still in the arctic, I think you'd be an alpha male."

Walter seriously doubted that. "Have you ever had a boyfriend, Dr. Stephanie?" he asked, an attempt to direct conversation away from himself.

She paused, frowned slightly.

Walter hated seeing her look like that. "Was it a bad question?"

"No, Walter. It's fine. I just—well...you've never taken an interest in that aspect of my life before."

"I'm interested in every aspect of your life, Dr. Stephanie."

She shrugged. "Relationships are overrated."

"But everybody needs somebody. You must have had somebody, too."

"Not really. Dr. Ron is the only human I interact with on a regular basis."

"That's a shame," said Walter.

She cocked her head. "What?"

He wished he hadn't said that aloud. He backtracked. "I mean...more. Wouldn't it be nicer to have more men around?"

"Probably, but sometimes I think the world would be better without men. Other times, I know it needs them."

"You hate men, Dr. Stephanie?"

"No, Walter, I don't hate them at all. I just don't know if I could ever be with one for an extended period of time."

"Are they bad to be around?"

"Not all of them. Guess I just haven't found one that I loved more than a monkey, or a moose, or a zebra..."

"You mean all animals?"

"Well, maybe not giraffes. It's something about their huge necks. I just don't like them."

Walter wasn't sure how to react to this, so he changed the subject. "How do you cope without love?"

"It's not that I don't have love, Walter. I love what I do. My job—and you, as part of it—is really the one thing that keeps me going."

"Me?"

"You serve a very important function in this pod, Walter. We wouldn't be up here if it weren't for you and the other animals. Men already know how to talk—too much—and how to interact with commercial and social worlds—and start wars and screw things up. There's no joy of discovery in them." She nuzzled him. "But there's plenty joy of discovery in you."

"There is?"

"Sure." She looked deeply into his eyes. Walter imagined he felt her soul; perhaps she was feeling his, too. "You know," she continued, "if I could marry a smart and handsome walrus like you, I think everything would be all right."

Walter started to engorge again. Residual embarrassment wilted it back to a flaccid state within seconds.

Dr. Stephanie's voice dropped to a near whisper. "Want to know a secret?"

He nodded.

"I've only kissed three things in my life, and one of those was my hamster, Toby."

"What's a hamster?"

"A rodent-like animal, kind of like a mouse, but different."

He squinted. "You kissed that?"

She looked away. "Maybe I shouldn't tell you this stuff."

71

"No, Dr. Stephanie. You should."

"Sorry, you just reminded me of my dad when you said that. He told me I shouldn't kiss animals, that they were dirty." She huffed. "He wasn't so clean himself, and what the hell did he know about animals? He used to throw my cat, Mittens, out of the house. Throw him, Walter!"

"It's inexcusable."

"That's right, Walter. You know more about justice and what's right than most people down there. I just think animals, as a whole, are better than people. I can't help it. But you have a point; it's good for a human to be around other humans. We're social animals, just like you."

Her words triggered thoughts within him. If that were the case, wouldn't it be good to have more walruses around, too? He imagined he'd like to be with another walrus—a guy walrus—and they'd hang out and shoot the shit and rub up and bang against one another at times, but mostly do guy stuff. "So, I should have another walrus to be friends with?" he asked.

Dr. Stephanie pursed her lips.

Walter goaded her. "Can you get another walrus for me?"

Finally, she said, "It isn't that easy, Walter."

"Will I *ever* get another walrus?"

"Honestly, probably not."

He wanted to sigh, but at least he didn't have to worry if he was to be the Alpha or Beta male. Alongside his training, Walter feared that type of social situation would prove too much for him. Still, it would be nice to have a friend with tusks.

"But I understand and share your emotions. It's lonely up here, so I'm glad I've got Dr. Ron."

Walter bristled.

Following a silent minute: "Well, we're all done." Dr. Stephanie gave him a quick toweling off. "Let's get you back to your room."

Feeling clean yet embarrassed, Walter flopped out of the shower.

HALL OF HORRORS

The space beasts' drug had stilled Space Walrus' body, but not his mind. He watched his illusory self run down an endless, featureless hall as the Inuit gave chase, followed closely by scores of scientists and product testers. Pulling up the rear, yet most fearsome of all: a gang of mutated walruses.

He tried to ignite his hyper-drive function, but his powers were useless here, and his body could only carry him so far. Collapsing, he waited for everyone to crowd and encircle him.

When they did, they left him little air to breathe, and what remained carried the stench of concentrated human.

"We've not yet begun to probe you," a scientist declared, clutching a pair of tongs.

"We have 634 new fragrances that must be on the shelves tonight!" shouted a tester.

"We saw him first!" an Inuit man retorted, "and we need him for our livelihood!"

Mutated walruses just growled and slobbered in the near distance.

Every hand reached for him. Space Walrus flailed, but fingers seized clumps of hide and held fast. A scientist produced a length of rope, tied him with it and pushed him to the floor. Hovering above, his captors seemed as tall as gods.

Inuit men began sharpening blades against dark shafts of flint. Scientists puzzled over charts and line graphs. A trio of product testers saw an opening and stepped up to Space Walrus. From decorative bottles, each sprayed something noxious in his face. "Is the pain unimaginable?" one asked.

"Yes!" he shouted, eyes smoking.

All three made notes in little black books.

Apart from the melee, a small team of scientists had set up an iron maiden, connected to various computerized pads and sensors. "Don't worry," one said, turning to Space Walrus. "It'll just monitor your biorhythms."

Then the Inuit stepped forward, tools and weaponry clutched in dark, chapped hands. Faces showed no emotion, at least none that Space Walrus recognized.

At that moment, a blood geyser erupted in front of him. An inhuman scent choked the air.

Mutated walruses had caught up with the humans. They sank fangs into scientists. Flayed the Inuit with mind-power alone. Rammed muddy claws through the bodies of product testers. There were so many creatures, lines upon lines of them that kept coming. In seconds, Space Walrus was the lone surviving non-mutant in the hall.

They closed in on him like the humans had done. He could feel their breath, somehow more substantial than mere air. Then the walrus felt their bodies, hot and sticky against his own. They smothered him, enveloped him in their physicality before reducing themselves to liquid. In it, Space Walrus began to drown.

It's not real, he thought to himself. *None of this is real.*

The sensible part of himself slowly returning, he wondered, distantly, if the space beasts had begun cutting yet, and if he would feel it when they did.

LATER THAT NIGHT

Walter listened closely. It was difficult to tell, but it seemed that someone was standing just outside his door.

There was a knock. He tensed. No one ever knocked after-hours.

Maybe, if he were quiet, whoever it was would go away.

Still, the knocking continued.

He wondered if it might be a zombie. Then he wished he'd never watched that movie, but it was just too good to turn away from. No other scary movie he'd seen had quite the impact of that one. Even the opening theme music made him want to hide his tusks under blankets, eyes peering out to see black and white horrors unfold onscreen.

"Hello?" Walter said.

The thing behind the door said nothing.

Zombies hardly ever spoke. It had to be a zombie. Suddenly, in his head, the entire film seemed to play at super-speed, over and over again. Now, Walter wished he'd never watched it.

The thing knocked.

He understood, at that moment, that it was not a regular zombie, but a smart one, one that remembered knocking on doors when alive—and it was coming for him and it was going to bite him, and if it didn't take too many bites—*partially devoured*, he remembered someone in the movie saying—then he'd become a zombie, too.

The door started to open, revealing a shaft of wan hall light. Walter was petrified. He wasn't ready to die, at least not via green and rotten teeth.

But it was just Dr. Stephanie.

Walter was doubly relieved. The shadows withdrew to darker parts of the room, but his heart didn't stop hammering in his chest for a good minute thereafter.

"Can I come in?" she asked, still in the hall, her upper body leaning into the room.

Walter was confused why she needed to ask. "Please," he said.

She entered then, took a seat on his pink bed. She looked at him; their eyes met. Walter wanted to break contact, but her attention held him captive. Finally, Dr. Stephanie spoke. "Sorry for coming so late, but I just wanted to make sure you felt better, after what happened earlier."

"Guess I'm over it," he said, though he wasn't over it at all.

"Good." After a slight pause: "You know, I've seen your penis before."

Walter shivered at the sound of that word. "Yeah, but you weren't expecting it to be so... big."

"True. But it really doesn't matter if you've got a hard-on, Walter."

"You don't have to put it so bluntly, Dr. Stephanie."

"And I don't mind seeing it. In fact, I like it."

Walter was dubious. "You do?"

"Yes, it reminds me that you are a true animal. Maybe even I forget that sometimes. No matter how many enhancements you get, never forget what you are, Walter. Keep it close to your heart, always."

"I will keep it very close to my heart."

She smiled. "Did you know there was an ancient religion that worshiped animals like gods?"

"Worshipped them how?"

"Carnally."

"You mean…"

She shook her head.

"Wow."

"Some think I'm crazy, but—working with Dr. Ron, and

learning about and talking with you—I know I'm not. I know I'm doing the right thing, what I'm meant to do."

"Glad to help," Walter said.

"This is so nice," Dr. Stephanie mused. "I can't speak my mind around just anybody—even Dr. Ron—and I'd have no reason to tell the chimps. They'd think I was bonkers. Well, most of them anyway."

Walter sensed he was getting to the heart of matters once secret. Mustering courage, he eventually felt brave enough to pose the important questions.

"So, why are you here, Dr. Stephanie? What is it you want?"

She looked askance at him. "You really want to know about my passion?"

"More than anything."

"Okay, then." With a nod, she started:

"I want voles to have a chance to raise their families in good neighborhoods and send their little vole children to good schools. I want vultures to give up scrounging for roadkill and settle down. And I want them paid competitive wages; I want them to become an integrated part of society. I want to see the first badger president."

The look in her eyes was electric.

"And I want to see the most patriotic animals serve their nations in battle."

"But how would all that work?" Walter asked.

"Animals would engage in jobs that are best suited for their bodies, with consideration given to their prosthetics and implants. They wouldn't be discriminated against and, like all mankind should, they'd be judged according to their actions and abilities. Who's to tell a vole he or she can't do road work or construction?"

"Do you think a walrus could ever be president?"

"I don't see why not," she said. "There will come a time of true equality, Walter. No more distinction between man and beast. We just look a little different, that's all. In twenty years, people will believe that, I promise you."

"Really? You promise?"

She paused, thinking to herself. "Well, in fifty years, at least. Then I can *definitely* promise you."

Walter ruminated. "I wonder what I'll be doing in fifty years."

Dr. Stephanie frowned. "Well, I—"

"And how old am I, anyway?"

"Seventeen," she said.

Images of *Sixteen Candles* and *The Breakfast Club* passed before his mind. "Wow, I'm a teenager!"

"Well, it's not the same in walrus years."

"Walrus years are different from people years?"

Dr. Stephanie nodded. "A lot different, yes."

"What exactly do you mean?"

"Nothing. I shouldn't have said anything."

Walter didn't intend to let this go. "No, really," he said. "What do you mean?"

She looked down at her lap, like she didn't feel comfortable making eye contact with him. "It's just that walruses don't have human life spans. On average, a human female will live thirty-seven years longer than a male walrus."

"That long?"

She nodded.

"I had no idea," he said. He wondered what it might be like to be dead. Lying in a casket, unable to open his eyes, unable to move, probably trapped in his poor, decaying self, which, if certain movies were to be trusted, was akin to a sleeping zombie.

Walter wanted to stop thinking such thoughts, but couldn't. "This is pretty heavy stuff, Dr. Stephanie."

"True, but consider it. Arthritis. Dementia. Cancer. Maybe it's a good thing you won't have to deal with such a long life."

Walter began to feel a little better.

"And there are things that have longer life spans than

humans. Take the Galapagos turtle. They can live for almost two-hundred years."

"I wonder how they spend those years," he mused.

"Fulfilling biological imperatives," said Dr. Stephanie.

Walter thought that was kind of sad, then kind of cool, just floating around in the water. That, he imagined, was sort of like floating in space, only more easily obtainable.

"Besides, you'll have a happier life than many poor humans down there. Some of them don't know the next time they'll eat."

"I guess you're right, Dr. Stephanie. I'm glad we had this conversation."

"I'm glad we did, too." She nuzzled him again. "Get some sleep. Conditioning comes early tomorrow."

"Okay. I will."

She motioned to the door. Walter squinted to make out her form in the darkness. "Dr. Stephanie?" he said.

"What?"

"Turn on the night light, please?"

She turned it on.

The walrus welcomed the escape from darkness.

A CHIMP ENCOUNTER
THE NEXT MORNING

Walter didn't want to go anywhere that he might encounter Dr. Stephanie. Their talk had helped, but what had transpired the night before still shamed him, made him feel vulnerable.

He was hungry, too. He hadn't eaten all day, and there was no more packaged food in his room. Salmon cakes would hit the spot. They were available on the station, but, to get them, he'd have to go to the cafeteria.

After swallowing apprehension, he decided to do just that.

Traversing the hall, Walter thought he heard footsteps. They weren't Dr. Stephanie footsteps—too small, too clipped, and there were too many of them.

The chimps.

He paused, listened. It sounded as though the footsteps were going off in the other direction, fading. Good.

Walter continued walking. Just as he turned the corner, he ran into a single-file line of primates. It fanned out across the hall. Crossing their arms, the chimps stared at him.

He grimaced. The bastards had been waiting all along, probably fooled him with false footsteps, too. A walrus' hearing wasn't the best.

"Hello, Walter," said Zapp.

"Hello," mimed Walter.

"Just wandering about, I see."

"I guess so."

"That's because it's all you can do around here, right?"

"Well, no. I—"

"He just doesn't want to admit he's useless," said Cosmo.

The chimps laughed.

Walter wanted to tell them to go fuck themselves—if not force them to make the sounds—but he didn't want to stoop to Dr. Ron's level.

"We're the opposite of useless," said Zapp. "Dr. Ron tells us we'll be heroes in a few years."

"And I've got an exclamation point in—" began Pow! before Zapp stomped his foot, shushing him.

Another added: "And we'll be sure to tell you all about the next space walk when we get back from it."

It was the first Walter had heard of this. "Space Walk?" he asked.

"Yeah, it's a real one, too. Some repairs to the station need to be made and *we're* going to make them."

Walter wanted to roar, but, as always, his voice was an electronic monotone. "I'll make them, too!" he said.

Again, the chimps erupted in laughter. It was getting to the point where Walter felt like his ears were bleeding whenever he heard that shrill, horrible sound.

"We got fitted for our space walk today," said Zapp. "Did you?"

"No, but—"

"Then you aren't going!" said Pow!.

Walter remained unmoved. "Did Dr. Ron say that? Did you ask him?"

"Didn't need to," said Zapp. "We know you're not going because you're *you*."

"Yeah," agreed Cosmo. "There was never a question about it."

Walter grumbled, "Then none of you know anything."

"Think about it," said Zapp. "They didn't let you do the practice walk. What makes you think you'll do the actual one? Face it, they'll never let a big, flabby animal perform delicate, sophisticated work."

"I can do whatever you can do!"

"In theory. Not in practice," said the chimp. "Can you do this?" He scratched his nose.

Defiantly, Walter scratched his own.

"No, stupid, I mean with a *real* hand."

The walrus slumped.

"If not for those fake things, you couldn't peel an orange," taunted Pow!.

"Totally useless," Cosmo concurred.

They had points, perhaps, but Walter couldn't let them destroy his hope. Come what may, he'd soon be a space hero, too. "No, Zapp, I'm doing the walk. Dr. Stephanie will tell you the truth."

"She will?" Zapp said.

Walter was resolute. "Yes."

The chimp extended a hand, bowed. "Then lead the way, Walter."

Turning awkwardly, he flopped toward Dr. Stephanie's office in a way he hoped exuded authority. Just behind him, Zapp sniggered. Then the other chimps started, too, and they walked slowly—like cripples or old men—just, it seemed, to mock him.

Walter burst through the double-doors to Dr. Stephanie's office. Dr. Stephanie jerked her head up, turned to Walter. He flopped into the room.

"Dr. Stephanie! Tell these assholes that I'm doing the space walk!" He had meant to say "chimps," but his converter translated the word he'd wanted to keep quiet in his brain.

Her eyes widened. "Walter! Watch your mouth!"

"I'm sorry, but these ass—chimps told me that I'd *never* go on a space walk." He turned to them. "But I am going, you furry fuckers! I am!" Though what came out of his voice converter was garbled, the gist was nevertheless discernable.

"Walter!"

"Just tell them the truth, Dr. Stephanie!"

Her angry look mellowed, her face forming an odd expression Walter couldn't read. Silently, she looked at—almost into—him. "Okay, Walter," she said, finally. "If that's what you want, I'll tell you."

Behind him, chimps sniggered again. His flippers started to tingle, in a bad way.

Dr. Stephanie looked over at the other animals. "You guys leave, okay? Go hang out with Dr. Ron."

"Come on," said Zapp. "We just wanna—"

More firmly: "I told you to go and hang out with Dr. Ron."

Acquiescing, several of the chimps chanced angry backwards glances at Dr. Stephanie before leaving the room. Out last, Zapp shot her a bird. Dr. Stephanie hadn't seen it, but Walter had. He squinted at the chimp; it was the most he could do.

The door latch clicked. With the chimps gone, the silence was oppressive.

"I'm sorry, Walter." Dr. Stephanie said.

He was perplexed. "Sorry for what?"

She sat down her pen, removed her reading glasses. "You won't be able to do it."

"*It?*"

"The space walk, I mean. But I really wish you could."

Walter was beyond flabbergasted. "Why not?" he wanted to roar. "I'm as capable as they are! I can do it! I'm smart enough! My hands work!"

"I know that, Walter."

"Then why won't you let me?"

"Because your body isn't made for a space walk."

The walrus was incredulous. "What?"

"Your tusks, Walter. Think about them."

"Do you disapprove?"

"It's not that. I—"

"They aren't the biggest or grandest, but they're mine!"

"That's not the point, Walter. We need to get a few more safety features installed, then you can go out into space."

"When will we get these *safety features?*"

"I can't say."

"You can't say?"

"I don't know."

"I thought you knew everything!"

"Well, it won't be anytime soon. I can say that."

"Dr. Stephanie, you're just dragging me along!"

"Don't think of it that way."

"What other way can I think of it? You promised me! You—"

Suddenly flustered, she shouted, "Just lay off it, Walter! We'll get them when we get them!"

He took a quick flop backwards.

Dr. Stephanie composed herself. "I'm sorry. I shouldn't have raised my voice like that."

"Are you...mad at me?" he asked, his prior anger all but forgotten.

"Of course I'm not mad. It's just that you've got to understand how things are."

"You still lied to me," Walter said.

"And I'm sorry for it. I knew you wanted to go out, but I couldn't find the heart to tell you it wouldn't happen."

"Would have been easier had you told me."

"Maybe you're right. But when we get the parts you can go out into space, even if I have to return to Earth and bring them up myself."

"Promise?"

"Cross my heart, Walter." She made the sign.

"Thank you, Dr. Stephanie. It means a lot. But I still want to float in space."

"And I want you there as well, but, again, it's not safe."

"I'll accept the risk," Walter said.

"That's very brave of you, but it's not up to me to decide.

It's up to Dr. Ron."

"Tell him to let me, Dr. Stephanie."

"But he's my superior." She half-smiled. "I really hope you understand. I can't break the rules for you."

"I do," he admitted. "I'm just disappointed."

"I know you are, but I want to make you feel better." She paused. "Remember when you mentioned wanting to do another zero-g session?"

Walter narrowed his eyes slightly. "I do," he said.

"Let's start one, right now."

"No. It's not *real.*"

"Come on, Walter. Let's get you into the simulator. You deserve it."

He wanted nothing more than to return to his room and mope, with no movies or music to interfere with his melancholic misery. "Maybe another day," he said.

"I'll go up with you this time."

Walter was too astounded to say anything more. His mind spun. Had she really meant it?

"You heard me," Dr. Stephanie said. "I'll have Dr. Ron man the controls."

That was all the confirmation Walter needed.

GOING UP

Dr. Ron was at the control station when they arrived. Walter looked over at him. The doctor grinned in a way the walrus interpreted as menacing, but Walter doubted he would do anything bad with Dr. Stephanie around. He wouldn't scare or hurt *her*.

The door closed. If Dr. Ron had plans to pull something, now would be the time he'd pull it.

Walter's apprehension faded when he and Dr. Stephanie left the ground. She placed her arms atop his shoulders as they rose higher and higher. The floor seemed very far away now, just like Walter's cares and concerns, which had crumbled to dust. He felt like pure energy. He *was* pure energy. He leaned backwards to let negativity exit his head in an imagined arc as he forgot all about gravity's shackles and curses. His mouth formed a smile of which he was unaware.

He imagined he was Space Walrus and she was Princess Stephanie. They were no longer in the simulator, but were floating weightless amongst the stars. No missions to run. They were merely spending quality time together, somewhere in the universe, far, far away from the closest planet.

"I've dreamed of a moment like this," Princess Stephanie said as Space Walrus twirled her like a ballerina.

"As have I," said Space Walrus, looking deeply into her eyes as she completed a pirouette.

"You mean that?" she asked.

"More than anything." He let her back bend over his flipper. When she leaned up, Princess Stephanie gave him a kiss on the lips.

Space Walrus felt a little spicy. When they began to tango, he took the lead. Her breath warmed his neck and shoulders as they danced on and on through the void.

Suddenly, Walter heard Dr. Stephanie's voice and realized it was coming from outside his head. He looked up at her through hazy, out-of-focus eyes.

She giggled. "You looked blissed out. Didn't want to disturb you."

"How long was I gone?"

"Over a minute."

"Really? It felt like a few hours."

"So, do you feel better about things now?"

He nodded. "A little. Dreams always make things better."

"I'm sorry things aren't the best for you, but they're going to improve soon. I promise." Suddenly, Dr. Stephanie floated nearer to Walter and spoke in a whisper beside his earflap. "I'm not supposed to say this. It's Top Secret."

"Top Secret?"

"Yes."

Not even the dream had seemed this big and all encompassing. Walter gave her his full attention.

"You're unique, Walter," she said, tone revelatory. "More unique than you know. We're saving the most special of all space walks just for you."

"What's going to be so special about it?"

"You'll have to wait and see." She stroked his head, the feeling like a static charge to his brain. "But it'll be worth it. You and I, we're going to make change together. Real change."

Walter's inner world was a storm of joy. "Really and truly?"

"Yes, Walter." She nuzzled him for longer than she had in months. "The chimps will be so jealous of you."

"You like me better than the chimps?" he asked, hopefully.

"Of course I do. Honestly, I don't think I could stomach another six years if you weren't the walrus you are. I love you, Walter. You're the sweetest thing on Earth."

"We're not on Earth."

Dr. Stephanie laughed at her flub. "In space, then." She leaned over and gave him a kiss.

"This is the happiest moment of my life, Dr. Stephanie!" Walter said, and meant it.

"Well, I'm glad I made you so happy. That's exactly what I came up here to do."

Slowly, they both descended to the bottom of the chamber. For Walter, this was usually a depressing time, but not with Dr. Stephanie at his side.

They reached the bottom. Dr. Ron eyed him as he stepped out of the simulator with Dr. Stephanie. Walter caught the glare, but turned back around. He had better things to focus on than Dr. Ron.

"Thanks so much, Dr. Stephanie," he said.

"No problem, Walter."

He closed the door to the simulator behind them after about thirty seconds spent maneuvering his backside around the corner.

Out in the hall, Dr. Stephanie went one way; he went the other.

If the chimps were gathered somewhere along his path, then so be it.

In his room, Walter closed his eyes, visualized himself as a sexy man with tusks. In his mind, this made his newfound image sexier. Betty—on the bed, as per usual—seemed to agree. She bunched the sheets around herself demurely, but Walter knew it was just part of the act. She was ready to show him everything she had to offer.

"What can I do for you, Walter?" she asked.

"You can polish my tusks," he said.

Walter brought forth the ball gag.

But the walrus on the bed wasn't a walrus anymore.

It was Dr. Stephanie; maybe it had always been Dr. Stephanie.

Horror threatened to deflate his penis. Arousal contradicted horror. He continued to masturbate.

He watched himself slip the ball gag over her mouth.

No!

Then he saw himself mount her.

Yes!

He had to stop, but couldn't. It felt so much better than it had when Betty was the fantasy object.

He entered her.

Dr. Stephanie was so warm inside, like freshly baked bread.

He splooged, hated himself, but that didn't stop the warm afterglow from settling over him, feeling like sunshine.

After pleasure had faded to a memory, Walter began to think things through. His lifespan was so much shorter than he had imagined. There was so little time to start doing things right, to impress Dr. Stephanie.

But what could he do? He was a fat, useless walrus. Everyone except Dr. Stephanie had told him that; maybe it was true.

No, he couldn't think that way. It was wrong. It was defeatist.

He had to become the walrus of his dreams. He had to make a stand—somehow, someway.

EMANCIPATION

Space Walrus still swirled in the muck of liquefied mutated walruses, but was no longer cowed. Will restored, he broke free from the hallucination and, for a time, entered a void.

Gradually, his eyes opened. The Head Vivisector was bent over him. The beast pulled on a flipper to gauge the optimum angle for incision, then turned it from side to side.

"Start wherever," Space Walrus said, slurring his words. "It's all good."

The Head Vivisector addressed the others, its voice a noxious combination of bubbling mud and skittering insects. Space Walrus assumed it had insulted him, as all the beasts began to laugh.

They mocked and derided the helpless, strapped down walrus.

They pointed at him, held up long, black fingers to their maws and pretended they were tusks.

They held their arms out to show him just how wide he was.

Space Walrus could stomach no more humiliation.

He let their mockery serve as fuel.

It became unadulterated strength and flowed through him unbridled, enlivening his mind, body and soul.

A renewed Space Walrus tossed off his tethers. He rammed the Head Vivisector in the eye with one of its own surgical instruments.

He grabbed another space beast, broke its hand off at the wrist.

He speared three of them with a single thrust of his tusks. Shaking his head back and forth, he dislodged them, their flying and flailing bodies knocking other beasts out cold.

As he flexed to show dominance, his muscles bulged obscenely.

Less than an Earth minute later, the last alien was dead.

Steaming black blood cascaded in runners down his body. Space Walrus unleashed a barbaric yalp that shook all things in the room and shattered glass beakers.

He only hoped he wasn't too late to save Princess Stephanie and spirit her away from this vile place.

Finally, he found her in another room, on another gurney.

She looked dead.

Space Walrus shed a tear.

Almost imperceptivity, her right eyelid began to flutter.

Maybe it was just his imagination, guided by sorrow.

But no, her chest was moving now. The breath of life was still within her.

Quickly, Space Walrus undid her straps, but she did not move, nor did she say anything. She just looked up at him.

At that moment, their inner beings met, and he felt like he was inside her eyes, and there he wanted to stay for the remainder of his days. It felt right. It felt destined.

Space Walrus continued staring.

Princess Stephanie gained enough strength to arise from the gurney.

"You gave me quite a scare," he said.

"I apologize."

"No need for that, my dear. You've been through hell."

"I owe you so much, but don't even know your name."

"It's Space Walrus."

She held out a hand; he kissed it. "I'm honored to meet you, Space Walrus."

"And I'm honored to stand beside such a woman," he said. "I sense your strength, Princess Stephanie. You have a warrior's spirit."

"I never gave up hope," she said.

"I admire that."

She bit her bottom lip, asked, "Can I give you a hug?"

"Of course."

Space Walrus and Princess Stephanie embraced. Her bosom was warm.

He pulled away. "Stay in this room until I return for you."

Her eyes widened. "You're leaving?"

"Sorry, but I must."

"Why?"

He looked toward the front of the ship. "Because there are things I must do."

A CALL FROM DR. RON

The phone blared. It seemed a malevolent thing to Walter, each ring portending black fate and ill omens.

He forced himself to move across the room and lift the receiver. "Hello, Dr. Ron," he said.

"Ah, you knew it'd be me."

"You're the only one who calls when I'm asleep."

"True, but I want you to know something, Walter. I'm through with being Mr. Nice Guy."

"You're not Mr. Nice Guy, Dr. Ron."

"Oh, you'll think I was after you see the stuff I've planned for you."

"What—what stuff?"

"I'll break off your tusks and shove them up your ass!"

"What did I do wrong, Dr. Ron? Tell me, please!"

"You'll rue the day you crossed me! Do you understand?"

"No, I—"

"I'm sick and tired of your games!"

Walter was dumbfounded. "What games?"

"I see the way you look, with those big, dumb eyes! I know what you're thinking!"

"I'm just a walrus!"

"I don't care what you are! Just lay the fuck off!"

"Lay the fuck off what?"

"Just do it!"

"Okay, I will!"

"Good." Dr. Ron's voice fell an octave, became gravely. "That's the right answer. The wrong answer would have left you in the rose garden."

"What rose garden? I—"

"Do you not think I have the balls for it? Let me assure you, I do."

"I know you have the balls, Dr. Ron."

"In the fucking rose garden, you asshole! That's where you'll be!"

"I said I know—"

"I don't give a *fuck* what you know, Walter!"

"You're really scaring me, Dr. Ron!"

"Just back off from Dr. Stephanie! Back off *now!*"

"Yes! I'm terrified and am shitting myself!" Walter said.

A laugh. "You'd better get used to shitting yourself. Day after day after day."

Walter could take no more. He slammed down the receiver, tried to daydream himself away from the memory of the conversation. Suddenly, he was Space Walrus, and the hero wandered through the bowels of a dark and foreboding house. He'd never been anywhere before but in space, and the walrus didn't seem very confident in his new surroundings. He trembled slightly when standing still. When moving, he just flopped on the ground, seeming fat and out of shape, much like Walter himself.

Suddenly, a dark form came up from behind Space Walrus. The form materialized into Dr. Ron. He pulled a bag around Space Walrus' head and kept it there as the animal thrashed. The bag fogged up with hot breath. His struggles grew weaker as Dr. Ron tugged on the plastic bag, drawing a limp body into the shadows.

Walter was ripped from the daydream by the sound of his voice converter, trying to scream. It took a minute before he understood there was no further threat, but even then he felt wordless, dazed. Never had a fantasy left behind such toxic residue.

He wondered if he'd dream about Space Walrus again, but Space Walrus was a special thing. No way could he die in some haunted house. No way could a man like Dr. Ron get the better of him, not even with the doctor's good looks, muscles and insanity. Space Walrus would be back for future adventures. Walter was sure of this.

THE NEXT DAY

Those fucking chimps.

Zapp leered. The rest of them leered, even Ray. Walter tried to ignore them, but they kept staring. "What do you want?" he asked, finally.

"We heard you coming—it's hard not to—so we thought we'd come out and say hello," Zapp said.

"Well, you said it," Walter muttered.

The chimp smirked. "Did you know Dr. Ron tells us *everything* about you?"

"He does?"

"Yeah. I bet we know more about you than you know about yourself."

Walter didn't like the arc of this conversation. "I'm not sure about that," he said.

"But I am. Just yesterday, in fact, he told us how often you masturbate."

Walter felt almost sick. "He told you... that?"

"Sure did. He says you whack it more than any animal he's seen." Zapp's eyes seemed to sparkle. "So, what is it you think about?"

"I—I—I, uh—"

"I bet I know." His grin was wide. "You've got a hard-on for Dr. Stephanie, don't yah?"

Cosmo chimed in: "Yeah, you want to see her naked!"

"Shut up!" Walter retorted, and was surprised he'd been so forceful.

"Just admit it. You know it's true."

"What I know is unknown, so blow it!" Walter wanted to

sigh. What was supposed to have been a killer put-down had been reduced to gibberish.

"It's obvious, Walter," Zapp continued. "You'd be putty in her hands, if she'd let you near them." The chimp looked him over. To Walter, his eyes felt like lasers. "Too bad she'd never go for such a fat slob."

"Not fat," Walter said. "Walruses have blubber."

"We know that, retard."

Walter understood he wasn't as smart or as sexy or as talented as the chimps, but did they have to keep reminding him of his inferiority? He shot back, "Dr. Stephanie says she likes walruses better than chimps!"

Zapp smirked. "Why should I care what she thinks?" He buffed his knuckles on his shirt. "Bet I could get her to do me."

Walter couldn't believe what he'd heard. His thoughts raced, so much so that the converter couldn't keep up with them. "You'll never do her! Dr. Stephanie wouldn't dream of doing a filthy monkey!" he'd tried to say. What came out: "No! Dr. Stephanie do no monkey! Filth!"

"I beg to differ. I know for a fact that Dr. Stephanie would go nuts for some monkey love."

"She would not!"

Zapp pressed Walter. "Has she ever kissed you?"

"Well, no…"

"But Dr. Ron has kissed us!" said Ray, suddenly.

Zapp turned, scowled at him. "No, Dr. Ron has not."

"Yeah," piped Pow! "He kissed me for the first time last year! Kissed me on the lips!"

Zapp spoke through clenched teeth, "Close those lips before I close them for you."

"One time, he called me Stephanie," said another chimp.

"Don't encourage him!"

"Can't you remember?" continued Pow! "He kissed us all. And one time, he even put—"

Zapp exploded. "Shut the fuck up, all of you! You are

never to talk of that and you know it!"

"But—" Pow! started.

Zapp slapped the shit out of Pow!. Walter had seen a man "slap the shit" out of someone in a movie and it looked very similar to what he'd just witnessed.

"But boss, it happened! It—"

Zapp didn't let him finish. Teeth bared, hands clutched into fists, he pounced upon and tore into Pow!'s body. Other chimps tried to approach Zapp, but his eyes were wild, filled with murder. "Get back!" he snarled.

The chimps retreated. "Lay off of him, Zapp! My god!" pleaded one from afar.

Walter could only stand there and watch.

Zapp came back to himself, but not before getting in a final slug to the jaw and a stomp to the junk. Pow! just trembled. Wide-eyed, staring at Zapp, he didn't even blink.

Finally, he said, "I deserved that. Thank you, Zapp." Peeling himself from the floor, Pow! tried to return to his room down the hall, but fell into the wall and slid down it.

Cosmo glared at Zapp. "If we hadn't stopped you, you might have killed him!"

Another: "Man, that wasn't cool."

"Fuck you, okay? And I'm no man!"

"But—"

"It never happened! *Never!*"

Zapp turned to Walter. "Just go," he said to him. "I'll catch up with you later."

THE BETRAYAL

For what felt like hours, Walter wandered the halls. He could not return to his room. He could not concentrate on movies or music. He did not feel the need to masturbate after what he'd seen and heard. All he could do was flop without thinking, without even registering the distasteful noise he made.

Down a darkened hall, Walter heard muffled voices.

He froze. He rarely heard humans in this area.

Walter approached the source, a room near the end of the hall.

Soon, he recognized the voices: Dr. Stephanie and Dr. Ron.

He flopped closer, stopping by a window to the right of the door. If he stretched, he could see into the room at just above desk-level. Quietly, Walter peered through the glass. He hoped no one would notice his eyes, or his orange rubber-topped head.

Inside, Dr. Ron loomed over Dr. Stephanie. It seemed he was going over the contents of a folder with her. Dr. Stephanie looked more tired than interested. Her hair was mused, her eyes puffy.

He wondered what she was thinking about.

Suddenly, Dr. Ron got up and turned from Dr. Stephanie, toward the door.

Walter flopped away hurriedly. The bend in the hall seemed so very distant, and he feared the man would hear his distinctive flops.

He reached the bend just as the door to the conference room opened.

He prayed Dr. Ron wasn't heading for him.

He listened close. It seemed he wasn't. Instead, Dr. Ron was visiting the bathroom across the hall.

A minute later, Walter heard a toilet flush, but didn't hear the sound of water pouring from a spigot. Then it sounded like Dr. Ron was leaving the bathroom. Moments later, the door—certainly the one behind which Dr. Stephanie waited—clicked shut, followed by an even fainter click of a lock.

Walter flopped from his hiding place back to the window.

Dr. Ron had returned to Dr. Stephanie, but no longer did he stand. He'd taken a seat close to her—too close, Walter thought. Dr. Ron seemed more interested in the woman than the folder she held.

What were they doing? What were they talking about?

Did she look happy? Agitated?

Was she there on her own free will?

He could only stare at her, wondering.

Dr. Ron tilted the folder back. Gradually, his face grew closer to Dr. Stephanie, his lips approaching her left cheek. Their flesh met. She didn't resist the touch, or even flinch slightly. In fact, she'd seemed to maneuver herself willingly in the direction of his lips.

Dr. Ron pulled away. She smiled at him.

Walter wanted to vomit. How could Dr. Stephanie do that? It would have been okay had she frowned or recoiled or smacked the man, but she *smiled*.

Hatred bloomed, yet the walrus did not bust down the door or confront both doctors. Instead, he turned around and flopped quietly back to his room. Every now and then, his voice converter turned thoughts into unwanted words:

"Fuck it all!"

"Damn it to hell!"

"Shit!"

Walter didn't even want his next scheduled bath.

The walrus paced back and forth across his tiny room. His

nerves were aflame. His mind was bathed in thoughts of betrayal.

How could she love a thing like Dr. Ron? Did the mere fact indicate that something was wrong with Dr. Stephanie? That she was a bad person, too? That she had been fooling him all these years, and that he was just a happy dupe?

Suddenly, Walter thought he understood how those tortured Shakespearean characters felt. Then it came to him: he needed to make her understand how *he* felt, and if that wasn't possible, then he needed to make her feel just as bad as he did, or even worse.

The harlot! Stab her with his tusks!

He made himself calm down.

He didn't want to kill her, but she had betrayed him, betrayed him so bad. For that, she would have to pay. There had to be some compensation for *him*.

A SAD BATH

Walter heard footsteps outside his door. When it opened, Dr. Stephanie entered the room, wearing Walter's favorite red-sequined swimsuit. He felt nothing upon seeing it.

"Hey, Walter. How's it going?"

The sound of her voice—so sweet in defiance of her act—triggered something in him. Maybe he didn't feel *nothing*. Maybe he felt jealousy, anger and spite. He wished walruses were capable of shooting venom from glands, like some other animals Dr. Stephanie had told him about.

A poisonous walrus would know how to deal with this situation.

"Are you ready for your bath?" she asked.

He made no reply.

"You look so gloomy today. Have a bad dream last night?"

"No," said Walter.

Her tone deepened. "Is that all I'm going to get from you?"

"Yes."

"Whatever, Walter. Just come on. Let's do this."

Walter got into position inside the shower. Dr. Stephanie took her customary seat.

She ran the sponge across the length of his back. The animal in him rippled. His eyes wanted to roll back. He wouldn't let them roll. That was just his body. To obey its whims would have left him feeling debauched. He couldn't allow himself to experience pleasure, not when it was given by those fingers and palms, attached to the body that had the cheek she'd let Dr. Ron kiss.

Now, she scrubbed with her hands. They felt like sandpaper. Then her fingers began to knead his hide. Prickles of warmth felt like daggers.

"I bet you feel all nice and relaxed now," she said.

Walter's voice converter made grumbling sounds, like water through clogged pipes.

Dr. Stephanie stopped scrubbing. She leaned over to face him. "You're really not relaxed, are you?"

"No, I'm not."

"You usually love baths. What's come over you, Walter?"

"Nothing," he said.

She dropped the sponge into the bucket, placed her hands on her hips. "Sounds like something to me."

If she was that oblivious, Walter figured she deserved his silence.

"Okay, let's finish this. Turn over so I can wash your underside."

Grudgingly, Walter turned.

Her hand scrubbed near his groin.

He winced.

"Isn't that better?"

"No."

"Come on, Walter. It's not hard to relax."

She was wrong. Relaxation was impossible when *truth* was building up inside him. "I can't!" he said, letting it out, then cursed his monotone and inability to vocalize rage. "I saw what you did!"

"What?"

"I saw what you did with Dr. Asshole!" He'd genuinely meant to say 'Dr. Ron.'

Dr. Stephanie frowned. "Dr. Asshole, eh? That's a new one."

"I saw you kiss him!"

She seemed startled. "I didn't kiss him," she said. "He kissed me."

"Why were you there with him?"

"I don't have to explain myself to you, Walter."

"You owe it to me."

She scowled, but said, "Okay. He called me in for a meeting. We looked over some charts and then he went to the bathroom. When he came back, he kissed me. It's as simple as that."

"But you let him!"

"Look, there's nothing between me and Dr. Ron."

"Then why did his lips touch your face?"

"Because he kissed it."

"Exactly, Dr. Stephanie!"

She waved him away. "Whatever, Walter. You shouldn't have been spying on us to begin with. I'm disappointed in you."

"Disappointed because I found out about you and Dr. Ron."

"Look, if you want me to say I'm sorry, then I'll say it."

"Good. You should be sorry."

Her look hardened. "I don't think I like your tone."

"Well, I don't think I like what you did!" Walter sneered at her. "Did his breath smell like ass, Dr. Stephanie?"

"Walter!"

"Were his lips slimy? Did they taste like slugs?"

Her face reddened. "Maybe his lips tasted good."

Walter couldn't have heard that right.

"Maybe I liked it when he kissed me," she continued.

He wanted to flush with rage.

"Maybe I'd like him to kiss me again."

"You harlot!"

"Call me what you like." She shot him a withering glance. "Again, it's none of your business."

"It *is* my business."

"And why is that?"

"Because I want you, Dr. Stephanie. In *that* way."

"What *way* are you talking about, Walter?"

For a change, he would assert himself. He would show her. Now. "Kiss me," he said.

"What?"

"Kiss me. It doesn't have to be on the mouth."

"No!"

"I've got a penile bone!"

"Walter—"

"Just do it, Dr. Stephanie. Kiss me."

She pulled away from him. "I won't!"

Walter felt like a ball of power, glowing brighter than the sun. Never could he be stopped. "Massage me, then."

"You mean—"

"Yes. Like you did that one time before."

"But I was just gathering your seed!"

His tone was icy. "Then gather it again."

Her tone was icy, too. "We're past that stage in research. We don't need more seed."

His eyes narrowed. "I'll never be touched again?"

"We might want a fresh sample in a few years."

"In a few years?"

"Walter, I—"

"No, I cannot accept this!"

She shook a fist at him. "You're being unreasonable!"

"In a few years, Dr. Stephanie? A few years? No! You're being unreasonable, you *bitch*!"

Dr. Stephanie looked pissed, if not enraged, but seeing her expression didn't hurt or confound Walter. It fueled his fire.

"Yeah," he said. "You heard me."

She threw the sponge at him. "You're being an asshole!"

"I'm not the asshole!" he exclaimed.

"Yes, you are!"

Walter could take no more. He rose up, dripping from his bath, and knocked Dr. Stephanie to the ground. Just short of mounting her, he slapped the back of her head with his flippers. He thought Dr. Stephanie might have said something, but Walter wasn't listening. His hard-on felt bronzed.

"Walter, stop!"

He returned to himself. Her voice sounded terrified, helpless. He looked past his rage, straight at her. Never had he seen her appear so hurt, then so furious.

"Get out!" she screamed. "Go!"

"But—"

She slapped his face.

"Dr. Stephanie! I—"

She slapped it again. Walter wanted to run to his room, hide from everyone, even himself, but he could only flop slowly away.

He'd done a terrible thing.

SPACE STORM

Space Walrus crashed his bulk into the door to the control room, smashing metal as if it were cheap wood.

Though the cockpit was filled with navigational equipment, the walls looked as cave-like as any other on the ship.

Space Walrus sat in the pilot's seat. The knobs and gauges seemed more organic than mechanical, but he was the smartest walrus of them all, so it didn't take long before he found the gear that turned the ship around, setting it on course to Princess Stephanie's home planet.

He heard footsteps behind him, tensed, and was ready to lash out with his tusks, but saw it was the princess.

"You shouldn't sneak up on me like that. My tusks are dangerous," he said.

She rubbed them. "They don't seem so dangerous to me."

"You don't know the places they've been, the things they've seen."

"Your tusks see things?"

"You know what I mean."

"I know they saved me."

Space Walrus grumbled. "I know I told you to stay in that room."

Her happy face fell. "Should I leave?"

"No," Space Walrus said. "Take a seat."

Princess Stephanie sat in the co-pilot's chair, reached for a button. "What does this do?"

"Just watch. Don't touch anything."

She looked crossly, if not knowingly, at him. "I'm smarter than you think," she said. "There's much you don't realize about yourself, Space Walrus, but not everyone's in the dark."

He turned slowly to her, his mouth uncharacteristically ajar. "Do you know about my past? My destiny?"

Princess Stephanie hesitated.

"Say something."

She shook her head. "I've said too much already."

"What do you mean?"

"Only my father knows the whole story, and only he can tell it."

Space Walrus wanted to press further—the secret of his identity was so close to being unraveled—but he'd noticed what appeared to be dots, hurtling through space. They looked unassuming, but the walrus knew better. He snarled and slammed his left flipper against the console.

"What's wrong?" Princess Stephanie asked.

"A shit-ton of asteroids," he said, "coming this way."

Moments later, the storm enveloped the ship, so many projectiles that space seemed to consist exclusively of hurtling things, some with tails of fire, others with rings of ice. The Princess covered her eyes. Space Walrus didn't flinch.

The ship took a blow to its left flank. It shook, listed, and Princess Stephanie slid sideways, out of the co-pilot's chair and into Space Walrus' lap.

"Will we make it?" she asked him.

He met her gaze. "What do you think?"

"I don't know. I—"

"Hush now."

"But—"

"Hush."

Turning from her, Space Walrus stared down the storm. If he could find its soul, he'd learn all about it. He'd mess with its mind and force it to dissipate. But the storm was defiant. It showed him only sharp nails and fangs.

He shrugged before pressing his foot to the gas and firing all boosters. Princess Stephanie gripped his hide as the ship screeched and groaned, bobbing above, below and between asteroids like a drowning swimmer in an angry sea.

A PHONE CALL FROM DR. RON

"Hey, Walter," said Dr. Ron.

"Hey," Walter replied, tentatively. He feared that Dr. Ron was calling to scold and berate him for assaulting Dr. Stephanie, to laugh at him for being so stupid as to think a beautiful woman could love a fat, useless walrus. Worse yet, Dr. Ron would probably inform him that Dr. Stephanie no longer wanted to work with walruses and that he—Dr. Ron—would be in charge of Walter from now on.

"I want to talk about Dr. Stephanie," said Dr. Ron.

Walter knew, at that moment, that his darkest fears had been verified.

"I want to talk about her with you, in depth."

"Yes, Dr. Ron. We can do that. Are you her boyfriend now? I know you love each other." Then he forced himself to say, "I'm very happy for you both."

Dr. Ron snorted. "It isn't me she wants. Don't you get it? It's you, you fat, tusked fucker!"

Walter's brain felt clogged; he didn't know what to say. Was Dr. Ron lying to him? Was this some sort of cruel trick? Walter choked out, "Me?"

"Yes, Walter! A hundred thousand times, yes!"

"You're wrong. Dr. Stephanie doesn't love me."

"But she does, Walter. She does. I try to make her love *me*, but all she talks about is you. Walter this and Walter that. Walter, Walter, Walter…"

"Are you shitting me?" He'd intended to say, "Are you serious?"

"What do you think? She wears those skimpy little outfits

when she exercises and bathes you. Has she ever worn them for me?"

Walter felt sick. He had slapped her with his flippers, and she *loved* him. "I don't know. I—"

"She hasn't, Walter! She hasn't and never will!"

"Maybe she will soon. Maybe—"

"Don't you dare try to make me feel better! I know the score! You know it, too!"

Walter didn't know what he knew, so he said nothing.

"It's not like I haven't already revealed too much of myself to you."

"You haven't revealed anything to—"

Dr. Ron shrieked, "I'll admit it, okay! I'll come clean! I'm only doing this because I'm jealous!"

"Of me?"

"Yes, you! You're fat and dumb! You've got a woman who'll feed and bathe you on a moment's notice! You've got the easy life, but you don't even know it! Fuck, I'd kill to be you!"

"But I'm not—"

"No, I really mean it. I'd *kill.*"

"Dr. Ron, I—"

"Hell, sometimes I feel like killing *myself.* Sometimes I feel like ending it all, right in the lab with Dr. Stephanie there, so she might finally know how much I love and need her. But then I think I should kill *her* for scorning me all these years. Kill her, myself—and take you with us!"

"What—what about your chimps?"

"What about them? I'd let them stay in the pod forever! I'd let them eat our corpses and then starve! I *hate* those black, furry *fuckers!*"

"Dr. Ron, my god!" Walter wanted to cry, though, in the back of his mind, he agreed that the chimps were *furry fuckers.*

"They've got it made, too, but do they show me respect?" Dr. Ron paused, as though anticipating Walter's answer.

He gave no reply.

"Well, they don't! They're just arrogant little primate pricks who haven't shown me love—real love—in over a month! A man has needs. Even you understand that, right?"

"I, uh, guess so," he said.

"They're all little bitches! Zapp especially! But he liked it before, Walter. He liked it and he begged for more, all night long." Dr. Ron paused, said in a lower voice, "Want to beg for more, Walter? All night long?"

"No, please," he said.

The doctor laughed. "Don't worry. I've no interest in your fat ass. Hell, I'm not much interested in anything anymore. The only things that bring me pleasure are alcohol and Dr. Stephanie. Can't have one, and I'm about to run out of the other until who-the-fuck-knows when, and it's so much better with booze, Walter. So much better. But next week, it'll be gone. Gone, Walter. And what will I do then?"

"I'm sure it's not that—"

"It is that *bad*, you arctic asshole! You know what it's like to live in my skin or walk in my shoes? You have no idea the sheer fucking agony that is my day-to-day life! You wouldn't last a minute breathing the air I breathe!"

"Calm down, Dr. Ron. It'll be okay. There'll be better days."

"Wrong! Better days are over, Walter! They've been over since the day I set eyes on your ugly mug!"

"I don't have a mug."

"You know what I'm talking about! I hate looking at your wrinkly anus-eyes! I hate it! And your face? God! Sometimes I want to—well, I just want to rip it off and see the gleaming white skull beneath!"

"Please, Dr. Ron! Please stop!"

Suddenly, his tone changed, softer now but more menacing. "It'd be easy to have an accident on this station," he said. "Maybe you're playing around and get yourself stuck in the airlock, and, god forbid, it opens. Bye-bye, Walter. Out you go. I'd watch for that kind of shit, if I were you."

"I'll be very careful," Walter said.

"Sorry. It won't matter how careful you are. You can't prevent it. I hold the key." He chuckled. "Should I open the lock, Walter?"

"I don't think—"

"Too late. I've already opened it. You might very well have that accident tomorrow."

He gulped.

"In fact, I'm sure you will."

Fear alone kept the receiver pressed against Walter's ear.

"But what sort of accident will it be?" Dr. Ron continued. "Maybe something heavy will fall on you. Maybe you'll eat something you shouldn't. I don't know, Walter. I'll have to think about it." The doctor yawned, and even that sounded terrifying to the walrus. "Well, that's all for tonight. See you tomorrow, rise and shine."

When Walter dropped the receiver, it missed the cradle. His flippers felt numb, his blood as cold as ice floes.

TERROR DAY

Walter awoke feeling pretty good—almost refreshed—before he remembered that he had destroyed his chances of having a relationship with Dr. Stephanie, and that this was the day Dr. Ron had scheduled him to die.

He turned on a movie, but couldn't concentrate. After turning it off, he stared at the stuffed walrus on his desk. When he'd watched the thing for long enough without blinking, it appeared to move, albeit slightly.

After a while, the illusion began to disorient him. Then it began to creep him out. He looked away quickly.

It didn't take him long to realize that he was hungry; he was always hungry when he first awoke. But what could he do about it? He had no choice but to remain forever in his cabin, melting into the bed.

But he had to eat something.

Walter peeled himself from the mattress. He rummaged through drawers and boxes in his room.

Eventually, he found half a cinnamon cookie in a bag and ate that. It was a little hard and somewhat musty tasting, but he'd eaten worse things in the past, including something pink and slimy that had been under his bed.

Still, the cookie helped for less than a half hour, and, in that time, Walter's thoughts continued to churn.

He became paranoid. He wished there was something large in the room that he could push up against his door. *No, that wouldn't help!* his mind screamed. *The door doesn't have hinges!*

Was an ancient cookie his last meal?

He couldn't let himself die on an empty stomach. Not

even convicted serial killers did that.

Maybe he could go quickly to the cafeteria, pick up a bag of chips and hurry back to his room. Dr. Ron was probably busy. The odds of running into him were slim.

But Dr. Ron had almost certainly dropped his work in favor of planning the ins-and-outs of murder.

Still, he had to try it, no matter what dangers the excursion posed. That's what Space Walrus would do. Space Walrus would stop at nothing to get to the cafeteria and eat to his heroic heart's content. If Walter hoped to become a space hero, he had to face down his fears.

Regardless, the walrus trembled as he stepped out into the hall. The lock on his door echoed slightly when it fastened. He cursed the noise and looked down the corridor, first in front of him, then behind. There was nothing.

Before going any farther, Walter peered up at the ceiling. He recalled Dr. Ron's threat concerning heavy objects and, in movies, had seen pianos drop from great distances onto the heads of people standing below. But there weren't any pianos hanging precariously above him.

Suddenly, he heard something. It didn't matter what that something was. He just knew he needed to hide from it.

Walter spotted an open broom closet. He ducked into it as quickly as his bulbous body allowed and closed the door behind him.

It was dark and cramped inside the closet. It smelled like disinfectant.

Walter's mouth itched; he didn't dare scratch it. He also hoped he wouldn't fart. Though his outbursts were infrequent, they were often quite loud.

Anus clenched tightly, Walter continued to listen. He heard multiple voices and realized that it wasn't Dr. Ron, but the chimps.

They passed by the closet. Walter could see them through the grating of the door. He just prayed they couldn't see him, too.

Quietly, barely breathing, he waited until he could no longer hear them. During that time, he had managed not to fart.

Opening the door, he looked around. Again, the hall was empty, but that brought little solace. It was usually easy to avoid Dr. Ron, but now Walter feared that he'd lurk behind every turn, or appear down one end of a hall only after Walter had traveled too far to turn back.

Still, the walrus continued to creep down the hall.

A moment later, just behind him, he heard something. It was the sound of a door opening. Not his imagination this time, for an arm emerged, ensnaring Walter before he could turn to see it snake around him.

The arm dragged the walrus into the room.

"Oh shit! Oh fuck! Oh shit! Oh fuck!" Walter couldn't prevent his voice converter from changing panicked thoughts into words.

"What are you oh shitting and oh fucking about?"

The walrus felt on the verge on panic, but Dr. Ron didn't seem agitated at all. In fact, he sat down at a desk and took a sip from the coffee cup in his hand. He said nothing as he regarded Walter, barely blinking.

"Are you going to bury me in the rose garden?" Walter asked.

Dr. Ron blinked. "No, Walter. I have no plans to do that."

Walter was too scared to be relieved. "You don't?"

"I don't." Dr. Ron patted his lap. "Come closer."

He hesitated.

"I just want to talk with you, one on one."

Reluctantly, the walrus obeyed.

"It's been a weird few days, hasn't it?" Dr. Ron said.

Walter could only nod at the understatement.

"But I'm through with all the drunken late-night phone calls. I'm sick of them, sick of myself!"

"What a relief," Walter meant to think, but said it instead.

Dr. Ron shrugged. "Whatever. I'll just have to be the bigger man, as I'm the only man here."

Walter didn't know what to say to this.

"And I'm not drunk like I was before, Walter. I'll have you know that. And I had an epiphany, too."

He'd heard that word in movies every now and then, but never understood what it meant. "What's that?" he asked.

"Imagine a bunch of broken pieces, coming together in a sudden blossoming of understanding."

He still wasn't sure what Dr. Ron was saying.

"To put it simply, it's to finally understand and come to grips with something, and I realized that I've been a pathetic man. I should *never* have let an animal get the better of me." He paused, eyes boring into the walrus. "It's sick, isn't it?"

"Yes," Walter said. "It's sick."

"So very sick, indeed."

Walter wished he could hide from Dr. Ron's eyes, yet the man kept them focused on him.

The doctor laughed at the walrus' discomfort. "It's like we're in a race, you and I—and we both know the prize at stake."

"Prize? Stake?"

He pounded a fist on the desk. "Dr. Stephanie, you assface!" Anger slid from him then; he looked almost forlorn. "She's so much younger than I am. Seven whole years."

"At least you won't die before you're thirty, Dr. Ron."

"That's not the point. The point is she doesn't need me and never will. So, I'm giving her to you, Walter." He lifted his hands, made a dusting motion. "She's all yours."

Walter was floored. "Wait. You can't—"

"I'm not the man I used to be. I've got crow's feet. My knees ache and my breath reeks. I'm over forty, for god's sake!"

Walter just stared.

"Don't look at me like that! I never thought it would come to this, but it has, and now I've got to deal with it like a man, and a man must make sacrifices."

Walter had no idea what to think, what to feel.

"Do you understand what I'm saying?"

"No. Not really."

Dr. Ron smiled. "Lean in closer, Walter. I have some secrets to tell you. They might help clear things up between us."

His words felt slithery in the walrus' ear.

"Dr. Stephanie told me she'd never go all the way with me, not as long as you were around."

"Then why does she fight me? And why doesn't she tell me these things?"

"She's shy. You've got to pry her out of her shell."

"But I don't know how to do that."

Dr. Ron seemed to think. "Your ultimate goal is to perform a space walk, right?"

Walter nodded.

"Dr. Stephanie would be *very* impressed if you'd do one of those."

"But that won't happen because you won't let me!"

"That was then, Walter." He paused, looked deep into the walrus' eyes. "What if I told you I could make it happen?"

"You can?"

"I can, and I will."

"What about the chimps? I thought——"

"Fuck them. They can wait."

Walter felt an odd sensation build up inside him. Maybe it was hope. "You're serious, aren't you?"

"Of course I'm serious, but I bet you don't have the balls to follow through. You're all talk and blubber."

"I have balls," Walter said.

Dr. Ron laughed. "Maybe you do, but you've got to prove it."

"I don't have to prove anything. I'm not your chimp."

"I didn't mean to *me*. I meant to Dr. Stephanie."

"Oh…"

Dr. Ron arched his brows, nudged Walter. "She'd totally make out with you," he said, "but only after a space walk."

"Did she tell you that?"

"No, but I can read her. Hell, I bet she'd even show you her titties."

"I—I don't know if I'd be ready for that. I—"

"Oh, you'll be ready once she shows you."

Walter felt conflicted. He feared Dr. Ron was luring him into a trap, but his dream of becoming a space hero, of Dr. Stephanie loving him, overpowered that fear.

"So," Dr. Ron continued, "if you've got the balls you say you have, then go out on that space walk and impress the fuck out of Dr. Stephanie. I'll okay it right here and now, no questions asked."

"But I don't think she'll allow it." A voice that told him Dr. Ron was lying prattled in his head. "Shut up!" Walter shouted at it, aloud.

Dr. Ron grimaced.

"I don't mean you! My converter messed up!"

He waved a dismissive hand. "Whatever. It doesn't matter what Dr. Stephanie says. I have seniority."

"What if something goes wrong?"

The doctor cocked his head. "Do you think something will go wrong?"

Walter considered it. A successful space walk would make Dr. Stephanie forget about their big fight. They could get married, have children and live happily ever after. A space hero and a brilliant scientist—they'd make the perfect couple.

Finally, he said, "No, I'm a Master of Space."

"That's right. You're a true master. Just think of the sights you'll see! Imagine the lands you'll conquer!"

"I don't want to think about conquering stuff."

"Consider whatever you like. Just do the space walk and claim what's yours. You can't fail, you blubbery asshole. It's your destiny."

"I guess it is," he said.

"So, you'll accept the challenge?"

Walter wished his converter could convey resoluteness. "Yes, Dr. Ron. I'll accept it."

He grinned. "Wonderful."

HOPE SPRINGS ETERNAL

In his room, Walter shined his tusks and studied himself in the mirror. When he smiled, he realized he'd not done so in over a day. How things had changed.

Looking down at his girth, he had to admit that even his blubber appeared more honed and muscular. Maybe it was actually something behind his eyes that indicated a new inner strength, something he hoped was tangible to others, and something he hoped Dr. Stephanie would recognize instantly.

But what if she didn't? What if she was still furious from last night? What if she smacked him a third time? What if he lost control and smacked *her*?

Walter pushed away such thoughts. He couldn't abide fear. He felt ready for anything. So ready, in fact, that he considered giving himself a wink in the mirror. Though he'd practiced with Dr. Stephanie, he still found winking difficult, and the way his implant simulated the act pulled hard at his eyelid and hurt.

No matter. It was time to make things known to the woman in his life.

Proudly, he walked down the hall toward Dr. Stephanie's office and opened her door.

She was hunched over, typing on a laptop that was on her desk.

"Hello, Dr. Stephanie," Walter said.

She didn't turn around. After an uncharacteristically long pause, she said, "Hello, Walter."

He asked, "Are you still mad at me, Dr. Stephanie?"

Her reply was curt: "I am."

"I did a bad thing; I know. But I'm not the same walrus

I was yesterday." He willed his lips to form a wide, beaming smile. "Do I seem any different to you?"

She glanced at him. "No," she said, and returned promptly to work.

He'd hoped she would at least sense his aura. "Are you sure?"

"Walter, I'm busy. I can't deal with you yet."

"Come on, Dr. Stephanie. Just look."

Eyes hard, she studied him. "You look the same as always. What are you trying to tell me?"

He had to unveil the news. It would make her forget all about what had happened the night before, and if he kept it corked much longer, he feared his very cells would implode. "I'm doing it!" he exclaimed. "I'm going on a space walk!"

Dr. Stephanie registered no surprise. No trace of joy, either. "Wrong, Walter," she said, coldly. "The chimps are doing it."

"Nope. They'll be in their cabin. Moping."

She shook her head. "Now you're babbling, Walter."

"But—"

"There's no way Dr. Ron's going to let you. And he's right. It's too dangerous for you out there. I already said we need additional safeguards first."

"He already okayed it, Dr. Stephanie."

"Impossible."

"I thought he was going to kill me, but instead he made me an offer."

"And why would he do that?"

"Because he loves you but doesn't deserve you. He realizes that now. He had an *epiphany*."

Her fingers drummed on the desk. "I'm so ashamed of you. You've jeopardized my professional relationship with Dr. Ron and all the work I've done with you. Humans are selfish, Walter, not walruses. Have you forgotten that?"

He flopped farther into the office, right up to her desk. "I *am* selfish," he said. "I'll do anything to keep Dr. Ron away from you."

Dr. Stephanie stood, pushed her chair back. She appeared ready to slap him again. Rather, she exhaled audibly and said, "You're not the walrus I used to know."

'You're not the Dr. Stephanie I used to know."

"Shut up, Walter."

"I will not, because I love you!"

She paused then, seemed to consider things. Walter hoped this was because he'd finally penetrated through to her. Closing her laptop, she walked past him toward the door. "Come with me. I'm going to prove that none of what you're saying is true."

In the hall, Walter had to quicken his pace to keep up with Dr. Stephanie. Usually, she walked at his speed. Not today.

They neared Dr. Ron's office. Walter wanted to burst headlong through the door in a show of male dominance and authority. Dr. Stephanie, however, charged through first. The walrus flopped in harmlessly behind her.

Dr. Ron sat at his desk, smiling, like he'd expected them.

"Dr. Stone, you won't believe what Walter just told me."

Walter had never heard Dr. Stephanie refer to Dr. Ron that way.

"He said he was going on the space walk in place of the chimps."

"Yes." Dr. Ron laced his fingers together. "That is correct."

Dr. Stephanie scowled at him, mouth slightly jar. "What?"

"Walter and I talked. We agreed that it was unfair to deny him any longer."

"See!" Walter said, happily. "I told you I was going!"

"Be quiet!" she shot back. Then she addressed Dr. Ron. "The repairs need to be done, yes, but they can wait another week, maybe longer."

"Walter goes tomorrow," he said, bluntly.

"But what if things go wrong?"

He shrugged. "We stand a good chance of losing him out there, sure."

Dr. Stephanie was nonplussed. "How can you shrug?"

"Plenty of animals have given their lives to science." He grinned at Walter. "History might even remember you for it."

She flushed. "He can't go without the safety features!"

"And you're well aware that we'll never get them!"

Those words lodged deep in Walter's brain. He turned to her. "Is that true, Dr. Stephanie?"

She shook her head sadly. "Yes, Walter. The technology is far beyond our budget."

"And unnecessary," added Dr. Ron.

Walter's eyes narrowed. Again, there was fire behind them. "Then you lied to me!"

"I didn't lie. I just couldn't break your heart."

"Well, it's broken now!"

"Maybe I was holding out hope for you. You understand that, right?"

"It doesn't matter. I'm going on the space walk, safety features or not."

Dr. Ron nodded. "If the worst happens, it won't be too big a loss. He's a third wheel and you know it."

Her eyes widened. "Walter is right here, you asshole!"

The insult didn't faze him. "If you worked with me and the chimps, you'd actually have something to show for all you've done," he said.

"But—"

"Sometimes it pays to be practical." He stood up from his desk, moved closer to her. "And I could certainly use your... expertise."

"He makes sense, Dr. Stephanie," Walter said.

Dr. Ron smiled. "See, even the walrus agrees. You're stuck with me for the next six years, Dr. Stephanie. You might as well make the most of it."

To Walter, as Dr. Ron loomed, she said, "Seriously, you don't need to do this. I'm already impressed with you, so very impressed."

"You are?"

Dr. Ron pointed a finger at her. "Don't try to talk him out—"

"Shut it, Dr. Ron!" Placing a hand on Walter's back, she said, "Wait here and I'll show you why." Dr. Stephanie arose then, turned towards her office.

Dr. Ron's eyes widened. He reached out, grabbed her shoulder. "You can't do that!"

She jerked away from him. "Like hell I can't!"

"I'm your superior!"

"If you can fuck your chimps, then I can tell Walter about his past!"

Dr. Ron blanched.

When Dr. Stephanie returned from her office, she carried something like a postcard in her hand. Something else protruded from a pocket of her lab coat. First, she showed Walter the object in her pocket—a small, walrus-shaped plushie. Dr. Ron frowned impotently as he watched.

"This is you," she said. "They sold thousands of these, mostly to schools."

Walter narrowed his eyes at it. "Doesn't look like me."

"But it is. Look at the tag. It says so right here."

"There could be other walruses named Walter."

"Don't you get it? You're the only walrus named Walter who's ever mattered!"

"I don't matter, Dr. Stephanie. Not yet."

Then she showed him a picture. Some middle-aged guy stood by a podium, waving. The first few rows of what seemed to be a huge crowd stretched in front of the man.

"Who is he?"

"That was the President of the United States."

"The guy who was blown up in that alien attack?"

"No, he was just the president in a movie."

Walter looked down at the picture. Beside the president, a young male walrus stood. "And who's that?" he asked.

"It's you, Walter."

"Me," Walter said, but not as a question.

"Yes, Walter, you. You don't have to do the space walk to be a space hero." She shook the picture in front of him. "You're already one!"

He wanted to shrug. "It doesn't matter unless I can be a space hero to you."

She bit at her lip, seemed almost desperate now. "Let me show you more."

"No, Dr. Stephanie. I—"

But she was already gone. When she returned from a second trip to her office, she'd lost the plushie and the picture and gained a thin stack of paperback books. She brought them over to Walter, got on her knees and began turning pages.

"Look, Walter! A series of children's books!"

"So what?"

She pointed at an illustration of a happy walrus in a white space suit. "You're the main character!"

"That doesn't look like me, either," he said. "Too cute."

"Don't you get it? I'm trying to make you understand how impressed everyone is with your story."

"Not me," muttered Dr. Ron.

"Can it!" she hissed.

Walter asked, "How many people are we talking about, Dr. Stephanie?"

"I don't know. Thousands. Maybe millions. You made a big impact."

Walter's tone was firm, resolute. "There could be a trillion of them and it'd still mean nothing."

"We're in agreement there, Walter," said Dr. Ron. "It means the same to me."

"Don't listen to him," Dr. Stephanie said. "I'm the only one here who wants what's best for you."

"But you'll still let me do the space walk, right?" Walter knew he needed to do it, not only to impress Dr. Stephanie, but also to set things right with himself.

Dr. Stephanie scrutinized him. "Nothing's going to stop you, is it?"

He shook his head.

"And you're never going to happy again until you do it?"

"That's right, Dr. Stephanie. I need to be complete."

"Okay, Walter. Okay."

BACK ON TERRA FIRMA

Though the storm had nearly pulled the ship apart, Space Walrus made it to Princess Stephanie's home planet. Immediately upon arrival, uniformed men whisked the princess away. When Space Walrus protested, he was told that doctors needed to examine her, and that the king awaited him.

Transportation to the castle had been arranged, but Space Walrus wanted a deeper experience of this new world. He'd started walking, instead.

The walrus marveled. The zone through which he traveled looked like the interior of a snow globe, writ large. It was a place where even the forests were draped with billowy gauze and white flakes fell constantly from the sky to be absorbed into the ground, more an endless stream of confetti than precipitation.

Still, the path to the castle was miles long. Space Walrus trudged to this destination until it loomed just before him, a fairytale dreamscape of white, fluted balustrades and parapets, flying buttresses galore.

He crossed the drawbridge over a mote filled with hot pink water. He imagined there might be cotton candy fishes within, but didn't look down.

Inside the castle, he found himself in a lobby so spectacular that it was too great for even his eyes. He could only see the room as *white*, with vague forms recognizable as tables or chairs.

It seemed that he was alone here. He waited.

The door across from him swung open. The king stepped

in, followed by regal consorts.

Trumpets blared.

"Welcome, Space Walrus! Welcome!"

The walrus bowed. When he arose, the king embraced him in an unanticipated hug. "I should bow to you!" he said. "I would be lost now, without my daughter."

"Don't thank me. I did what I was asked to do, nothing more."

"But surely you deserve something."

"I wish to accept no credit for this."

"You are too humble." The king moved to a long table. Sat down. He gestured to the nearest chair. "Take a seat, Space Walrus. Now that you've succeeded in your mission, I have much to tell you."

He took a seat.

The king leaned in closer. "These are things you've wondered about for years, so listen well."

Space Walrus absorbed the king's every word. What he said sounded crazy, but, somehow, it felt true.

The king continued, "Though your mother was an Earth-bound walrus, your father was a walrus from my planet, on a scientific mission that got...sidetracked."

"By passion?" Space Walrus said.

He nodded. "Their union was consummated and a son was born. You, Space Walrus, are that son."

"You mean—"

"Yes."

"What happened to my parents?"

"They grew happy together, died at ripe old ages."

"Good. But what does the past mean for me now?"

"Look down at your favorite tattoo."

Space Walrus did. He was amazed to see that it had changed. The rock was there, but the walrus was gone. In its place, Princess Stephanie sat, and she was smiling, not a tear in either eye.

"You are the one destined to take my daughter's hand in marriage."

It seemed unreal to him. A wife? But he was Space Walrus, constant vagabond and warrior. Could he cope with such a radically different pace and lifestyle?

There was but one place he could go to find the answer to such personal questions.

Stilling his thoughts, the walrus closed his eyes and dove into the center of his being. There, he touched and linked with the golden, burning thing that was his innermost soul. The resulting ecstasy erased all doubt from his mind.

"Now do you understand?" said the king.

Space Walrus opened his eyes. "I understand," he said. "I understand everything."

"And you will accept the hand of Princess Stephanie?"

"Only a fool would reject it."

"Indeed. But you must pass a final test before the ceremony commences."

"Name it."

"You must again venture out into the blackness of space and there unravel the Great Mystery of Life. Only that will fulfill prophecy."

Space Walrus wasn't fazed. "I see," he said.

"Will you need to prepare first?"

"No, I'm ready now."

"Then I wish you the best of luck."

"No need for wishing, my good king; I shall not fail you," Space Walrus said, and soared up into space, to swim among the lonely stars and discover the true meaning of everything.

THIS IS GROUND CONTROL

Walter was taken, for the first time ever, to a whole new pod. He wanted to marvel, but it looked almost exactly the same as Pod 10. Perhaps other, more interesting things were secreted behind closed doors.

The room to which they brought him resembled a cramped, technologically advanced dressing chamber.

Walter had little time to spare before work started on him. Men who he'd never met began wiping him down and then fitting his bulky walrus body into a space suit. They tugged sleeves over his electro-arms. He'd never felt so many hands on his tail.

There were holes for his tusks, and those holes were sealed with metal rims and screws after the ivories had been guided through them.

Once the initial fitting was complete, Walter was able to relax as the men worked on sealing certain areas of his suit.

He imagined himself as Space Walrus. The man in charge became more than just the guy who was suiting him up. He was now The Glorious Emperor. The men beside him: his pink leotard-wearing consorts.

The Glorious Emperor draped a golden breastplate atop Space Walrus' chest. On the breastplate: an insignia of a badger devouring a serpent.

The walrus removed it. "I cannot accept this, for I am already the honorary king of a beautiful world named Walrusonia."

"Good Space Walrus, you can be both king of Walrusonia and emperor of our humble domain."

"But it will seem boastful," he said.

"Nonsense," replied the emperor. "It's only boastful if the gift wasn't deserved."

"Then I, Space Walrus, shall accept!"

Trumpets blared, angels sang, and, from speakers high up in the clouds, the opening chords of *Space Oddity* wafted.

"You're ready to go now," said one of the men fitting him out.

Walter was jarred from his fantasy. "Just give me one second, please," he said.

"Okay, buddy. Whatever you say."

And then he was back.

Space Walrus stood outside the balcony, waving at those who would soon be his loyal subjects. The crowd leapt to hysterics; he basked in its energy.

The daydream having reached a suitable finale, Walter returned to himself.

"Thanks." he said, smiling at the men. "That was all I needed."

SAY GOODBYE

The chimps had all gathered out in the hall to see Walter off.
Dr. Ron stood rigidly in front of his protégés. He did not make
eye contact with the walrus, but, every now and then, glanced
over at Dr. Stephanie. She returned each glance angrily, and he
looked away.

The chimps remained silent. Dr. Ron bopped Zapp's
shoulder. "Congratulate him!"

"Hell no! I ain't gonna—"

He bopped him harder, spoke through clenched teeth and
pursed lips: "You can and you will."

"Why do I have to be the ambassador? Why not Ray?"

"Don't be an uppity little bitch. You know who controls
you. Now congratulate him!"

Ray grinned.

"But—"

Dr. Ron reared back his hand, like he intended to hit Zapp.

"Congratulations, Walter," he squeaked.

"There," Dr. Ron said. "That wasn't so bad, was it?"

The chimp trembled. Dr. Ron's expression became one of
contentment.

"You can all go now," Dr. Stephanie said, finally.

"Excuse me?" said Dr. Ron.

"I need some time alone with Walter."

All but Zapp and Dr. Ron turned to leave the room.

"I meant everyone," she continued.

Zapp huffed, kicked a foot, but left anyway.

"Damn it, I meant you too, Dr. Ron!"

"Come on, Dr. Stephanie. Can I just—"

"No!"

Head down, he left the room, too.

Dr. Stephanie turned to Walter. She got on her hands and knees before him. "Please," she said, "don't go."

"I've already made up my mind, Dr. Stephanie."

"But think of what might happen—"

"I'm ready for whatever comes."

"Are you sure of that?"

"With all my heart, hope to die."

"Don't say that, Walter."

"But I mean it, Dr. Stephanie," he said. "Today will be great. Don't worry."

"That's not easy. You're my Walter." She placed her hand on his flipper. "I just wish you'd stay in here, where it's warm."

"But there's no glory where it's warm."

"Maybe you don't need glory. Maybe you—" Dr. Stephanie choked. A tear rolled from her right eye, then from her left.

"Aren't you proud of me?" he asked.

"Of course," she said. "I'm very proud of you."

"Then why are you crying?"

She wiped her eyes. "I'm just a little scared, that's all."

"There's no need for fear."

Dr. Stephanie hugged him then. "I can't help it. You're everything to me."

"You're everything to me, too, Dr. Stephanie." He paused. "And you mean it? We're still friends?"

Silently, she nodded.

"And you forgive me for the terrible thing I did?"

"Maybe I'm partially to blame."

"No, Dr. Stephanie, it was all my fault."

She broke the hug. "I want you to hear something, Walter, and I want you to believe it, too."

He narrowed his eyes. "What?"

"I didn't mean it when I said that I liked the way Dr. Ron's kiss felt."

"You didn't?"

"No, I hated it."

When Walter smiled, Dr. Stephanie gave him a kiss. It was too warm and loving to be erotic. He melted into it.

"Just be careful out there," she said. "Do it for me."

For just a moment, Walter saw her as Princess Stephanie. "Don't worry, your highness," he said. "I would die before letting you down."

As Walter turned to the airlock, he heard her say, "Goodbye, Walter."

"Call me Space Walrus," he said.

Dr. Stephanie's bottom lip trembled. "Then goodbye, Space Walrus."

As Walter listened to her retreating footsteps, he realized now was the time to seize his destiny. He just hoped Dr. Stephanie would be at the window, watching. He'd blow her a kiss.

SPACE WALK

The airlock opened. Walter floated into space, swallowed by blackness that was too big and scary. It seemed a living, breathing thing, and it reminded him that he was a fat, lazy blob, not at all prepared for what was at hand.

Walter hoped to see Dr. Stephanie watching him—that would bring comfort—but there weren't any windows on this side of the station. He turned to the airlock, but it had already closed. There was no way to open it from the outside.

Now, everything around him, skin especially, felt tight. The chimps had been right about him. He had to get back to plain steel walls and his pink bed. There was no other choice.

He made himself think brave, rational thoughts.

You're here, Walter. This is where you've always wanted to be. Now enjoy yourself, damn it!

Yes. This experience brimmed with possibilities. He was floating in space—actual, honest-to-god space, where no walrus had gone before. He was an innovator, a trailblazer. The first of his kind. Fear vanished as he gave himself freely to the moment.

I'm living my dream.

That meant something. No. That meant *everything*.

He felt without body. He was weightless. He forgot all that he'd been told of the mission, thought of Space Walrus instead and welcomed him into his heart.

Empty space was now populated by space beasts, and they were coming at him from all sides, all dimensions.

Whatever, Space Walrus thought. *Let them come.*

He swung his mighty tusks at them, severing the first beast's head in single swoop. Then he reared forward, gored another through the stomach and out its back. Space Walrus had to shake the guts from his body. A dripping, red spine was wedged between his tusks.

It was brutal, certainly, but being a Master of Space meant acting with fearless spontaneity. It meant accepting the fact that violence was a sad but necessary evil.

Suddenly, from a twisty, red gun, the beasts shot ropes of stringy, molten flesh towards him. Like snakes, they took on life, tried to encircle and bind him.

Space Walrus ripped at the tethering coils.

Walter pulled himself from the waking dream just long enough to realize that his tusks had severed his cord.

He tried to spin around, as quickly as possible, to grab the cord with electro-hands and hope they had enough strength to pull him back to the airlock. But the cord already seemed miles away. It floated out in front of him like a starched spaghetti strand.

Fuck, he thought, and his converter vocalized it.

The chimps, he knew, were watching, somehow—watching and laughing.

No, don't think of them!

But it was hard not to think of the chimps and a thousand other terrible things. There seemed to be no outside reality; he had only his body and his mind to occupy him, and he heard just his breaths—in and out, in and out. He'd never before paid much attention to the sound they made, so deep and raspy.

Spinning again, he saw his station. It looked so far away now, just a vague, doughnut-shaped thing all but swallowed by an oily sea.

The reality of his situation began to sink in.

I'm going to die soon.

He'd just go back to his fantasy. Yes. Go back into it for as long as it took the blackness to swallow him completely.

No matter how he tried, Walter could not conjure up another Space Walrus dream. Instead, he imagined what it would feel like with his suit off. So cold—cold like the arctic, cold like his old home on the floe. He could almost remember it, the tastes and smells, the simple, wordless communion with other tusked animals, and smaller, slick ones for which he then had no name. There was no music, no movies—just pure walrus-hood, and when he looked up, he imagined that he was in the cold water, and there was ice above him, and he was about to break out of it into the light of day.

But there was no ice, just the vast eternity of space.

That wasn't so bad, was it? Maybe he no longer needed to dream about Space Walrus. Maybe he'd become Space Walrus. He wasn't floating away from the ship or Dr. Stephanie.

No.

He was in total control.

He was a Master of Space.

It was okay; everything was fine. In fact, it was *awesome*, even better than being back in the station or some barely remembered home. And it no longer mattered to him that his physical body would stop working soon. He'd become spirit and maybe, after a time, would reincarnate on Earth, and there'd be another woman in his life. Ultimately, he would discover that she was the reincarnation of Dr. Stephanie, and would remind her of their past lives. They would fall in love all over again, plan and start a family, have children—half-human, half-walrus hybrids who would herald the beginning of a new age of equality.

In some way, Dr. Stephanie would always be there.

She would remain with him forever.

Loving him.

And, amazingly, she was there now. He saw her floating, suit and helmet-free, in the vastness of open space. Her image filled up the entirety of Walter's vision.

"Dr. Stephanie?" he said.

She said nothing, just smiled and enfolded him in an embrace that felt like everything, until everything fell away and became nothing at all.

EPILOGUE

Dr. Stephanie and Walter were in bed, the covers coiled around them. Though the walrus still slept, light through the window told her that morning had arrived.

Reaching out, she touched Walter, letting her hand glide gently down his back.

He awoke with a start, but his frown turned just as quickly into a smile, and he nuzzled her. How Dr. Stephanie relished the soft touch of his lips and the coarse bristle of his vibrissae. The dueling textures never ceased to stimulate her.

"Want some breakfast?" she asked.

"Not now," he said.

"Aren't you hungry?"

"I am hungry, yes," he replied, his voice neither monotone nor electronic. "Hungry for you."

Stephanie was ready for him; she was always ready. Turning over, he mounted her, his body feather-light.

Dr. Stephanie awoke as Walter entered her.

With an ache, she realized Walter was dead—had been so for over twenty years—and an orangutan, not a walrus, slept quietly beside her. His name was Ward. Interspecies marriage had been made legal, thanks in no small part to the work she'd done on the space station and back on Earth, years afterward.

She and Ward had been married for a score. He was soft-spoken. He was dependable. When together, they smiled for others and attended expensive parties. His friends liked her, or at least she thought they did. More importantly, however, she was successful. Life was good; she was living her dream, and barely did she think of Walter during those first few years after her and Ward's honeymoon.

But the orangutan had changed. He wasn't as fast as he used to be—mentally, physically, or sexually. Dull golden fur looked patchy in places, and each time she'd feel the texture of his skin, she felt walrus flesh, instead.

She'd been having an affair for the last three years. She didn't know if Ward knew. He'd never said anything, and she'd never cared to ask.

Briefly, and almost absent-mindedly, she imagined herself placing a pillow over his head, holding it there.

Though Ward was a heavy sleeper, Stephanie crawled carefully over him to the edge of the bed. There, she sat for a while, listening to her husband's snores before standing. A knee popped; her back felt stiff.

Walking to a window, she looked out. There were no streetlights on this side of the house; she saw only darkness, darkness like space.

Inside, she felt hollow. She'd only understood Walter's love for space after she left it, the pull towards it growing stronger and more insistent as time passed. But she didn't really yearn for it—or for escape in general—until she realized, completely and utterly, that she'd ran out of love for Ward. Then thoughts of Walter came pouring back, and—during bad nights—she couldn't stop the flood.

Perhaps this was another bad night.

Gripping the facing, she stared wistfully up at the moon and the blackness to all sides of it, and somewhere in that endless blackness was Walter, her Space Walrus.

Or had his body re-entered Earth's orbit to come crashing down like a meteorite?

No. She had to believe he was still there, in stasis, looking exactly how he did so many years before, just colder. And perhaps, past infinite miles of blackness, there was another opening to this world, another way in, and though he might not wear the same face, or even be a walrus again, Walter would find it, and she would sense him when he did.

For the time being, her breath fogged the glass.

Thoughts spiraled into regret. If only she could have come to terms with things then. If only she had been stronger and truer to herself. Now, she could only look up at the stars and think of being back in Pod 10, but with no Dr. Ron, no chimps. It would be as if they never existed, and she would be Princess Stephanie, reigning with her Space Walrus, again and always.

ABOUT THE AUTHOR

Kevin L. Donihe, perhaps the world's oldest living wombat, resides in the hills of Tennessee. He has published seven other books via Eraserhead Press. His short fiction and poetry has appeared in Psychos: Serial Killers, Depraved Madmen, and the Criminally Insane, The Mammoth Book of Legal Thrillers, ChiZine, The Cafe Irreal, Poe's Progeny, Bathtub Gin, Not One of Us, Dreams and Nightmares, Electric Velocipede, Bust Down the Door and Eat All the Chickens, and many other venues. He also edits the Bare Bone anthology series for Raw Dog Screaming Press, a story from which was reprinted in The Mammoth Book of Best New Horror 13.

Visit him online at facebook.com/kevin.l.donihe

BIZARRO BOOKS

CATALOG   SPRING 2012

ERASERHEAD PRESS

Your major resource for the bizarro fiction genre:

WWW.BIZARROCENTRAL.COM

Introduce yourselves to the bizarro fiction genre and all of its authors with the Bizarro Starter Kit series. Each volume features short novels and short stories by ten of the leading bizarro authors, designed to give you a perfect sampling of the genre for only $10.

BB-0X1
"The Bizarro Starter Kit" (Orange)
Featuring D. Harlan Wilson, Carlton Mellick III, Jeremy Robert Johnson, Kevin L Donihe, Gina Ranalli, Andre Duza, Vincent W. Sakowski, Steve Beard, John Edward Lawson, and Bruce Taylor. **236 pages $10**

BB-0X2
"The Bizarro Starter Kit" (Blue)
Featuring Ray Fracalossy, Jeremy C. Shipp, Jordan Krall, Mykle Hansen, Andersen Prunty, Eckhard Gerdes, Bradley Sands, Steve Aylett, Christian TeBordo, and Tony Rauch. **244 pages $10**

BB-0X2
"The Bizarro Starter Kit" (Purple)
Featuring Russell Edson, Athena Villaverde, David Agranoff, Matthew Revert, Andrew Goldfarb, Jeff Burk, Garrett Cook, Kris Saknussemm, Cody Goodfellow, and Cameron Pierce **264 pages $10**

BB-001"The Kafka Effekt" D. Harlan Wilson — A collection of forty-four irreal short stories loosely written in the vein of Franz Kafka, with more than a pinch of William S. Burroughs sprinkled on top. **211 pages $14**

BB-002 "Satan Burger" Carlton Mellick III — The cult novel that put Carlton Mellick III on the map ... Six punks get jobs at a fast food restaurant owned by the devil in a city violently overpopulated by surreal alien cultures. **236 pages $14**

BB-003 "Some Things Are Better Left Unplugged" Vincent Sakwoski — Join The Man and his Nemesis, the obese tabby, for a nightmare roller coaster ride into this postmodern fantasy. **152 pages $10**

BB-004 "Shall We Gather At the Garden?" Kevin L Donihe — Donihe's Debut novel. Midgets take over the world, The Church of Lionel Richie vs. The Church of the Byrds, plant porn and more! **244 pages $14**

BB-005 "Razor Wire Pubic Hair" Carlton Mellick III — A genderless humandildo is purchased by a razor dominatrix and brought into her nightmarish world of bizarre sex and mutilation. **176 pages $11**

BB-006 "Stranger on the Loose" D. Harlan Wilson — The fiction of Wilson's 2nd collection is planted in the soil of normalcy, but what grows out of that soil is a dark, witty, otherworldly jungle... **228 pages $14**

BB-007 "The Baby Jesus Butt Plug" Carlton Mellick III — Using clones of the Baby Jesus for anal sex will be the hip sex fetish of the future. **92 pages $10**

BB-008 "Fishyfleshed" Carlton Mellick III — The world of the past is an illogical flatland lacking in dimension and color, a sick-scape of crispy squid people wandering the desert for no apparent reason. **260 pages $14**

BB-009 "Dead Bitch Army" Andre Duza — Step into a world filled with racist teenagers, cannibals, 100 warped Uncle Sams, automobiles with razor-sharp teeth, living graffiti, and a pissed-off zombie bitch out for revenge. **344 pages $16**

BB-010 "The Menstruating Mall" Carlton Mellick III — "The Breakfast Club meets Chopping Mall as directed by David Lynch." - Brian Keene **212 pages $12**

BB-011 "Angel Dust Apocalypse" Jeremy Robert Johnson — Meth-heads, man-made monsters, and murderous Neo-Nazis. "Seriously amazing short stories..." - Chuck Palahniuk, author of Fight Club **184 pages $11**

BB-012 "Ocean of Lard" Kevin L Donihe / Carlton Mellick III — A parody of those old Choose Your Own Adventure kid's books about some very odd pirates sailing on a sea made of animal fat. **176 pages $12**

BB-015 "Foop!" Chris Genoa — Strange happenings are going on at Dactyl, Inc, the world's first and only time travel tourism company. "A surreal pie in the face!" - Christopher Moore **300 pages $14**

BB-020 "Punk Land" Carlton Mellick III — In the punk version of Heaven, the anarchist utopia is threatened by corporate fascism and only Goblin, Mortician's sperm, and a blue-mohawked female assassin named Shark Girl can stop them. **284 pages $15**

BB-027 "Siren Promised" Jeremy Robert Johnson & Alan M Clark — Nominated for the Bram Stoker Award. A potent mix of bad drugs, bad dreams, brutal bad guys, and surreal/incredible art by Alan M. Clark. **190 pages $13**

BB-031 "Sea of the Patchwork Cats" Carlton Mellick III — A quiet dreamlike tale set in the ashes of the human race. For Mellick enthusiasts who also adore The Twilight Zone. **112 pages $10**

BB-032 **"Extinction Journals" Jeremy Robert Johnson** — An uncanny voyage across a newly nuclear America where one man must confront the problems associated with loneliness, insane dieties, radiation, love, and an ever-evolving cockroach suit with a mind of its own. **104 pages $10**

BB-037 **"The Haunted Vagina" Carlton Mellick III** — It's difficult to love a woman whose vagina is a gateway to the world of the dead. **132 pages $10**

BB-043 **"War Slut" Carlton Mellick III** — Part "1984," part "Waiting for Godot," and part action horror video game adaptation of John Carpenter's "The Thing." **116 pages $10**

BB-047 **"Sausagey Santa" Carlton Mellick III** — A bizarro Christmas tale featuring Santa as a piratey mutant with a body made of sausages. 124 pages $10

BB-048 **"Misadventures in a Thumbnail Universe" Vincent Sakowski** — Dive deep into the surreal and satirical realms of neo-classical Blender Fiction, filled with television shoes and flesh-filled skies. **120 pages $10**

BB-053 **"Ballad of a Slow Poisoner" Andrew Goldfarb** — Millford Mutterwurst sat down on a Tuesday to take his afternoon tea, and made the unpleasant discovery that his elbows were becoming flatter. **128 pages $10**

BB-055 **"Help! A Bear is Eating Me" Mykle Hansen** — The bizarro, heartwarming, magical tale of poor planning, hubris and severe blood loss...
150 pages $11

BB-056 **"Piecemeal June" Jordan Krall** — A man falls in love with a living sex doll, but with love comes danger when her creator comes after her with crab-squid assassins. **90 pages $9**

BB-058 **"The Overwhelming Urge" Andersen Prunty** — A collection of bizarro tales by Andersen Prunty. **150 pages $11**

BB-059 **"Adolf in Wonderland" Carlton Mellick III** — A dreamlike adventure that takes a young descendant of Adolf Hitler's design and sends him down the rabbit hole into a world of imperfection and disorder. **180 pages $11**

BB-061 **"Ultra Fuckers" Carlton Mellick III** — Absurdist suburban horror about a couple who enter an upper middle class gated community but can't find their way out. **108 pages $9**

BB-062 **"House of Houses" Kevin L. Donihe** — An odd man wants to marry his house. Unfortunately, all of the houses in the world collapse at the same time in the Great House Holocaust. Now he must travel to House Heaven to find his departed fiancee. **172 pages $11**

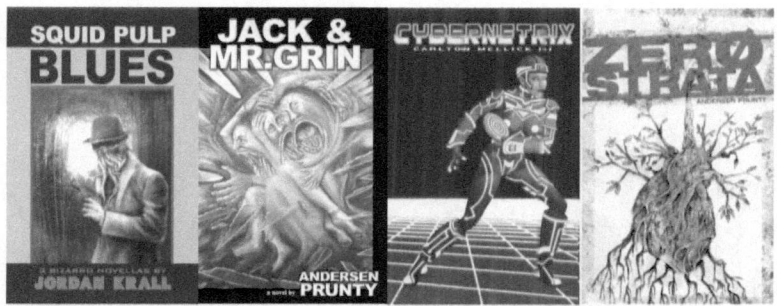

BB-064 **"Squid Pulp Blues" Jordan Krall** — In these three bizarro-noir novellas, the reader is thrown into a world of murderers, drugs made from squid parts, deformed gun-toting veterans, and a mischievous apocalyptic donkey. **204 pages $12**

BB-065 **"Jack and Mr. Grin" Andersen Prunty** — "When Mr. Grin calls you can hear a smile in his voice. Not a warm and friendly smile, but the kind that seizes your spine in fear. You don't need to pay your phone bill to hear it. That smile is in every line of Prunty's prose." - Tom Bradley. **208 pages $12**

BB-066 **"Cybernetrix" Carlton Mellick III** — What would you do if your normal everyday world was slowly mutating into the video game world from Tron? **212 pages $12**

BB-072 **"Zerostrata" Andersen Prunty** — Hansel Nothing lives in a tree house, suffers from memory loss, has a very eccentric family, and falls in love with a woman who runs naked through the woods every night. **144 pages $11**

BB-073 "The Egg Man" Carlton Mellick III — It is a world where humans reproduce like insects. Children are the property of corporations, and having an enormous ten-foot brain implanted into your skull is a grotesque sexual fetish. Mellick's industrial urban dystopia is one of his darkest and grittiest to date. **184 pages $11**

BB-074 "Shark Hunting in Paradise Garden" Cameron Pierce — A group of strange humanoid religious fanatics travel back in time to the Garden of Eden to discover it is invested with hundreds of giant flying maneating sharks. **150 pages $10**

BB-075 "Apeshit" Carlton Mellick III - Friday the 13th meets Visitor Q. Six hipster teens go to a cabin in the woods inhabited by a deformed killer. An incredibly fucked-up parody of B-horror movies with a bizarro slant. **192 pages $12**

BB-076 "Fuckers of Everything on the Crazy Shitting Planet of the Vomit At smosphere" Mykle Hansen - Three bizarro satires. Monster Cocks, Journey to the Center of Agnes Cuddlebottom, and Crazy Shitting Planet. **228 pages $12**

BB-077 "The Kissing Bug" Daniel Scott Buck — In the tradition of Roald Dahl, Tim Burton, and Edward Gorey, comes this bizarro anti-war children's story about a bohemian conenose kissing bug who falls in love with a human woman. **116 pages $10**

BB-078 "MachoPoni" Lotus Rose — It's My Little Pony... *Bizarro* style! A long time ago Poniworld was split in two. On one side of the Jagged Line is the Pastel Kingdom, a magical land of music, parties, and positivity. On the other side of the Jagged Line is Dark Kingdom inhabited by an army of undead ponies. **148 pages $11**

BB-079 "The Faggiest Vampire" Carlton Mellick III — A Roald Dahl-esque children's story about two faggy vampires who partake in a mustache competition to find out which one is truly the faggiest. **104 pages $10**

BB-080 "Sky Tongues" Gina Ranalli — The autobiography of Sky Tongues, the biracial hermaphrodite actress with tongues for fingers. Follow her strange life story as she rises from freak to fame. **204 pages $12**

BB-081 "Washer Mouth" Kevin L. Donihe - A washing machine becomes human and pursues his dream of meeting his favorite soap opera star. **244 pages $11**

BB-082 "Shatnerquake" Jeff Burk - All of the characters ever played by William Shatner are suddenly sucked into our world. Their mission: hunt down and destroy the real William Shatner. **100 pages $10**

BB-083 "The Cannibals of Candyland" Carlton Mellick III - There exists a race of cannibals that are made of candy. They live in an underground world made out of candy. One man has dedicated his life to killing them all. **170 pages $11**

BB-084 "Slub Glub in the Weird World of the Weeping Willows" Andrew Goldfarb - The charming tale of a blue glob named Slub Glub who helps the weeping willows whose tears are flooding the earth. There are also hyenas, ghosts, and a voodoo priest **100 pages $10**

BB-085 "Super Fetus" Adam Pepper - Try to abort this fetus and he'll kick your ass! **104 pages $10**

BB-086 "Fistful of Feet" Jordan Krall - A bizarro tribute to spaghetti westerns, featuring Cthulhu-worshipping Indians, a woman with four feet, a crazed gunman who is obsessed with sucking on candy, Syphilis-ridden mutants, sexually transmitted tattoos, and a house devoted to the freakiest fetishes. **228 pages $12**

BB-087 "Ass Goblins of Auschwitz" Cameron Pierce - It's Monty Python meets Nazi exploitation in a surreal nightmare as can only be imagined by Bizarro author Cameron Pierce. **104 pages $10**

BB-088 "Silent Weapons for Quiet Wars" Cody Goodfellow - "This is high-end psychological surrealist horror meets bottom-feeding low-life crime in a techno-thrilling science fiction world full of Lovecraft and magic..." -John Skipp **212 pages $12**

BB-089 "Warrior Wolf Women of the Wasteland" Carlton Mellick III
— Road Warrior Werewolves versus McDonaldland Mutants...post-apocalyptic fiction has never been quite like this. **316 pages $13**

BB-091 "Super Giant Monster Time" Jeff Burk — A tribute to choose your own adventures and Godzilla movies. Will you escape the giant monsters that are rampaging the fuck out of your city and shit? Or will you join the mob of alien-controlled punk rockers causing chaos in the streets? What happens next depends on you. **188 pages $12**

BB-092 "Perfect Union" Cody Goodfellow — "Cronenberg's THE FLY on a grand scale: human/insect gene-spliced body horror, where the human hive politics are as shocking as the gore." -John Skipp. **272 pages $13**

BB-093 "Sunset with a Beard" Carlton Mellick III — 14 stories of surreal science fiction. **200 pages $12**

BB-094 "My Fake War" Andersen Prunty — The absurd tale of an unlikely soldier forced to fight a war that, quite possibly, does not exist. It's Rambo meets Waiting for Godot in this subversive satire of American values and the scope of the human imagination. **128 pages $11**

BB-095 "Lost in Cat Brain Land" Cameron Pierce — Sad stories from a surreal world. A fascist mustache, the ghost of Franz Kafka, a desert inside a dead cat. Primordial entities mourn the death of their child. The desperate serve tea to mysterious creatures. A hopeless romantic falls in love with a pterodactyl. And much more. **152 pages $11**

BB-096 "The Kobold Wizard's Dildo of Enlightenment +2" Carlton Mellick III — A Dungeons and Dragons parody about a group of people who learn they are only made up characters in an AD&D campaign and must find a way to resist their nerdy teenaged players and retarded dungeon master in order to survive. 232 **pages $12**

BB-098 "A Hundred Horrible Sorrows of Ogner Stump" Andrew Goldfarb — Goldfarb's acclaimed comic series. A magical and weird journey into the horrors of everyday life. **164 pages $11**

BB-099 "Pickled Apocalypse of Pancake Island" Cameron Pierce—A demented fairy tale about a pickle, a pancake, and the apocalypse. **102 pages $8**

BB-100 "Slag Attack" Andersen Prunty— Slag Attack features four visceral, noir stories about the living, crawling apocalypse. A slag is what survivors are calling the slug-like maggots raining from the sky, burrowing inside people, and hollowing out their flesh and their sanity. **148 pages $11**

BB-101 "Slaughterhouse High" Robert Devereaux—A place where schools are built with secret passageways, rebellious teens get zippers installed in their mouths and genitals, and once a year, on that special night, one couple is slaughtered and the bits of their bodies are kept as souvenirs. **304 pages $13**

BB-102 "The Emerald Burrito of Oz" John Skipp & Marc Levinthal —OZ IS REAL! Magic is real! The gate is really in Kansas! And America is finally allowing Earth tourists to visit this weird-ass, mysterious land. But when Gene of Los Angeles heads off for summer vacation in the Emerald City, little does he know that a war is brewing...a war that could destroy both worlds. **280 pages $13**

BB-103 "The Vegan Revolution... with Zombies" David Agranoff — When there's no more meat in hell, the vegans will walk the earth. **160 pages $11**

BB-104 "The Flappy Parts" Kevin L Donihe—Poems about bunnies, LSD, and police abuse. You know, things that matter. **132 pages $11**

BB-105 "Sorry I Ruined Your Orgy" Bradley Sands—Bizarro humorist Bradley Sands returns with one of the strangest, most hilarious collections of the year. **130 pages $11**

BB-106 "Mr. Magic Realism" Bruce Taylor—Like Golden Age science fiction comics written by Freud, *Mr. Magic Realism* is a strange, insightful adventure that spans the furthest reaches of the galaxy, exploring the hidden caverns in the hearts and minds of men, women, aliens, and biomechanical cats. **152 pages $11**

BB-107 "Zombies and Shit" Carlton Mellick III—"Battle Royale" meets "Return of the Living Dead." Mellick's bizarro tribute to the zombie genre. **308 pages $13**

BB-108 "The Cannibal's Guide to Ethical Living" Mykle Hansen— Over a five star French meal of fine wine, organic vegetables and human flesh, a lunatic delivers a witty, chilling, disturbingly sane argument in favor of eating the rich.. **184 pages $11**

BB-109 "Starfish Girl" Athena Villaverde—In a post-apocalyptic underwater dome society, a girl with a starfish growing from her head and an assassin with sea anenome hair are on the run from a gang of mutant fish men. **160 pages $11**

BB-110 "Lick Your Neighbor" Chris Genoa—Mutant ninjas, a talking whale, kung fu masters, maniacal pilgrims, and an alcoholic clown populate Chris Genoa's surreal, darkly comical and unnerving reimagining of the first Thanksgiving. **303 pages $13**

BB-111 "Night of the Assholes" Kevin L. Donihe—A plague of assholes is infecting the countryside. Normal everyday people are transforming into jerks, snobs, dicks, and douchebags. And they all have only one purpose: to make your life a living hell.. **192 pages $11**

BB-112 "Jimmy Plush, Teddy Bear Detective" Garrett Cook—Hard-boiled cases of a private detective trapped within a teddy bear body. **180 pages $11**

BB-113 "The Deadheart Shelters" Forrest Armstrong—The hip hop lovechild of William Burroughs and Dali... **144 pages $11**

BB-114 "Eyeballs Growing All Over Me... Again" Tony Raugh— Absurd, surreal, playful, dream-like, whimsical, and a lot of fun to read. **144 pages $11**

BB-115 **"Whargoul" Dave Brockie** — From the killing grounds of Stalingrad to the death camps of the holocaust. From torture chambers in Iraq to race riots in the United States, the Whargoul was there, killing and raping. **244 pages $12**

BB-116 **"By the Time We Leave Here, We'll Be Friends" J. David Osborne** — A David Lynchian nightmare set in a Russian gulag, where its prisoners, guards, traitors, soldiers, lovers, and demons fight for survival and their own rapidly deteriorating humanity. **168 pages $11**

BB-117 **"Christmas on Crack" edited by Carlton Mellick III** — Perverted Christmas Tales for the whole family! . . . as long as every member of your family is over the age of 18. **168 pages $11**

BB-118 **"Crab Town" Carlton Mellick III** — Radiation fetishists, balloon people, mutant crabs, sail-bike road warriors, and a love affair between a woman and an H-Bomb. This is one mean asshole of a city. Welcome to Crab Town. **100 pages $8**

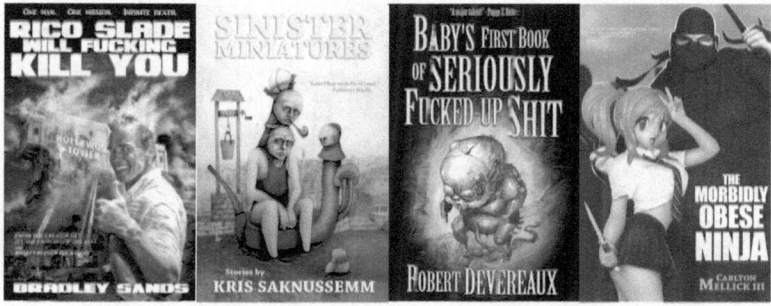

BB-119 **"Rico Slade Will Fucking Kill You" Bradley Sands** — Rico Slade is an action hero. Rico Slade can rip out a throat with his bare hands. Rico Slade's favorite food is the honey-roasted peanut. Rico Slade will fucking kill everyone. A novel. **122 pages $8**

BB-120 **"Sinister Miniatures" Kris Saknussemm** — The definitive collection of short fiction by Kris Saknussemm, confirming that he is one of the best, most daring writers of the weird to emerge in the twenty-first century. **180 pages $11**

BB-121 **"Baby's First Book of Seriously Fucked up Shit" Robert Devereaux** — Ten stories of the strange, the gross, and the just plain fucked up from one of the most original voices in horror. **176 pages $11**

BB-122 **"The Morbidly Obese Ninja" Carlton Mellick III** — These days, if you want to run a successful company . . . you're going to need a lot of ninjas. **92 pages $8**

BB-123 "Abortion Arcade" Cameron Pierce — An intoxicating blend of body horror and midnight movie madness, reminiscent of early David Lynch and the splatterpunks at their most sublime. **172 pages $11**

BB-124 "Black Hole Blues" Patrick Wensink — A hilarious double helix of country music and physics. **196 pages $11**

BB-125 "Barbarian Beast Bitches of the Badlands" Carlton Mellick III — Three prequels and sequels to *Warrior Wolf Women of the Wasteland.* **284 pages $13**

BB-126 "The Traveling Dildo Salesman" Kevin L. Donihe — A nightmare comedy about destiny, faith, and sex toys. Also featuring Donihe's most lurid and infamous short stories: *Milky Agitation, Two-Way Santa, The Helen Mower, Living Room Zombies,* and *Revenge of the Living Masturbation Rag.* **108 pages $8**

BB-127 "Metamorphosis Blues" Bruce Taylor — Enter a land of love beasts, intergalactic cowboys, and rock 'n roll. A land where Sears Catalogs are doorways to insanity and men keep mysterious black boxes. Welcome to the monstrous mind of Mr. Magic Realism. **136 pages $11**

BB-128 "The Driver's Guide to Hitting Pedestrians" Andersen Prunty — A pocket guide to the twenty-three most painful things in life, written by the most well-adjusted man in the universe. **108 pages $8**

BB-129 "Island of the Super People" Kevin Shamel — Four students and their anthropology professor journey to a remote island to study its indigenous population. But this is no ordinary native culture. They're super heroes and villains with flesh costumes and out-landish abilities like self-detonation, musical eyelashes, and microwave hands. **194 pages $11**

BB-130 "Fantastic Orgy" Carlton Mellick III — Shark Sex, mutant cats, and strange sexually transmitted diseases. Featuring the stories: *Candy-coated, Ear Cat, Fantastic Orgy, City Hobgoblins,* and *Porno in August.* **136 pages $9**

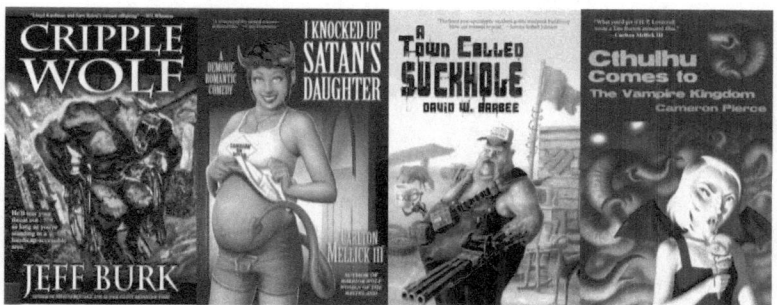

BB-131 **"Cripple Wolf" Jeff Burk** — Part man. Part wolf. 100% crippled. Also including *Punk Rock Nursing Home, Adrift with Space Badgers, Cook for Your Life, Just Another Day in the Park, Frosty and the Full Monty*, and *House of Cats*. **152 pages $10**

BB-132 **"I Knocked Up Satan's Daughter" Carlton Mellick III** — An adorable, violent, fantastical love story. A romantic comedy for the bizarro fiction reader. **152 pages $10**

BB-133 **"A Town Called Suckhole" David W. Barbee** — Far into the future, in the nuclear bowels of post-apocalyptic Dixie, there is a town. A town of derelict mobile homes, ancient junk, and mutant wildlife. A town of slack jawed rednecks who bask in the splendors of moonshine and mud boggin'. A town dedicated to the bloody and demented legacy of the Old South. A town called Suckhole. **144 pages $10**

BB-134 **"Cthulhu Comes to the Vampire Kingdom" Cameron Pierce** — What you'd get if H. P. Lovecraft wrote a Tim Burton animated film. **148 pages $11**

BB-135 **"I am Genghis Cum" Violet LeVoit** — From the savage Arctic tundra to post-partum mutations to your missing daughter's unmarked grave, join visionary madwoman Violet LeVoit in this non-stop eight-story onslaught of full-tilt Bizarro punk lit thrills. **124 pages $9**

BB-136 **"Haunt" Laura Lee Bahr** — A tripping-balls Los Angeles noir, where a mysterious dame drags you through a time-warping Bizarro hall of mirrors. **316 pages $13**

BB-137 **"Amazing Stories of the Flying Spaghetti Monster" edited by Cameron Pierce** — Like an all-spaghetti evening of Adult Swim, the Flying Spaghetti Monster will show you the many realms of His Noodly Appendage. Learn of those who worship him and the lives he touches in distant, mysterious ways. **228 pages $12**

BB-138 **"Wave of Mutilation" Douglas Lain** — A dream-pop exploration of modern architecture and the American identity, *Wave of Mutilation* is a Zen finger trap for the 21st century. **100 pages $8**

BB-139 **"Hooray for Death!" Mykle Hansen** — Famous Author Mykle Hansen draws unconventional humor from deaths tiny and large, and invites you to laugh while you can. **128 pages $10**

BB-140 **"Hypno-hog's Moonshine Monster Jamboree" Andrew Goldfarb** — Hicks, Hogs, Horror! Goldfarb is back with another strange illustrated tale of backwoods weirdness. **120 pages $9**

BB-141 **"Broken Piano For President" Patrick Wensink** — A comic masterpiece about the fast food industry, booze, and the necessity to choose happiness over work and security. **372 pages $15**

BB-142 **"Please Do Not Shoot Me in the Face" Bradley Sands** — A novel in three parts, *Please Do Not Shoot Me in the Face: A Novel*, is the story of one boy detective, the worst ninja in the world, and the great American fast food wars. It is a novel of loss, destruction, and--incredibly--genuine hope. **224 pages $12**

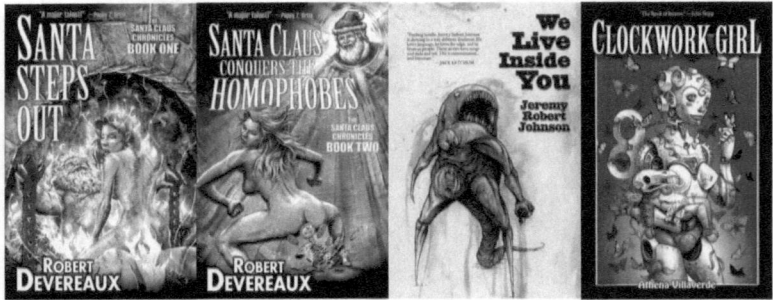

BB-143 **"Santa Steps Out" Robert Devereaux** — Sex, Death, and Santa Claus ... The ultimate erotic Christmas story is back. **294 pages $13**

BB-144 **"Santa Conquers the Homophobes" Robert Devereaux** — "I wish I could hope to ever attain one-thousandth the perversity of Robert Devereaux's toenail clippings." - Poppy Z. Brite **316 pages $13**

BB-145 **"We Live Inside You" Jeremy Robert Johnson** — "Jeremy Robert Johnson is dancing to a way different drummer. He loves language, he loves the edge, and he loves us people. These stories have range and style and wit. This is entertainment... and literature."- Jack Ketchum **188 pages $11**

BB-146 **"Clockwork Girl" Athena Villaverde** — Urban fairy tales for the weird girl in all of us. Like a combination of Francesca Lia Block, Charles de Lint, Kathe Koja, Tim Burton, and Hayao Miyazaki, her stories are cute, kinky, edgy, magical, provocative, and strange, full of poetic imagery and vicious sexuality. **160 pages $10**

BB-147 **"Armadillo Fists" Carlton Mellick III** — A weird-as-hell gangster story set in a world where people drive giant mechanical dinosaurs instead of cars. **168 pages $11**

BB-148 **"Gargoyle Girls of Spider Island" Cameron Pierce** — Four college seniors venture out into open waters for the tropical party weekend of a lifetime. Instead of a teenage sex fantasy, they find themselves in a nightmare of pirates, sharks, and sex-crazed monsters. **100 pages $8**

BB-149 **"The Handsome Squirm" by Carlton Mellick III** — Like Franz Kafka's *The Trial* meets an erotic body horror version of *The Blob*. **158 pages $11**

BB-150 **"Tentacle Death Trip" Jordan Krall** — It's *Death Race 2000* meets H. P. Lovecraft in bizarro author Jordan Krall's best and most suspenseful work to date. **224 pages $12**

BB-151 **"The Obese" Nick Antosca** — Like Alfred Hitchcock's *The Birds*... but with obese people. **108 pages $10**

BB-152 **"All-Monster Action!" Cody Goodfellow** — The world gave him a blank check and a demand: Create giant monsters to fight our wars. But Dr. Otaku was not satisfied with mere chaos and mass destruction.... **216 pages $12**

BB-153 **"Ugly Heaven" Carlton Mellick III** — Heaven is no longer a paradise. It was once a blissful utopia full of wonders far beyond human comprehension. But the afterlife is now in ruins. It has become an ugly, lonely wasteland populated by strange monstrous beasts, masturbating angels, and sad man-like beings wallowing in the remains of the once-great Kingdom of God. **106 pages $8**

BB-154 **"Space Walrus" Kevin L. Donihe** — Walter is supposed to go where no walrus has ever gone before, but all this astronaut walrus really wants is to take it easy on the intense training, escape the chimpanzee bullies, and win the love of his human trainer Dr. Stephanie. **160 pages $11**